INN *in* ABINGDON

Donnie Stevens

Inn in Abingdon

© 2011

Donnie Stevens

ISBN: 978-1-936553-04-4

This book is a work of fiction.
Names, characters and incidents are products
of the author's imagination. Any similarity to actual
people and / or events is purely coincidental.

Warwick House Publishers
720 Court Street
Lynchburg, Virginia 24504

Acknowledgments

Cover Photo: 1865 photo of Martha Washington College courtesy of the Historical Society of Washington County, Virginia.

Original flower image credit: www.forestwander.com

To Kevin Edwards for your work in crafting the beautiful cover for Inn in Abingdon. Kevin, it's awesome.

To Lona Kokinda for creating a photo of me for the cover. Thanks for making me look good.

To a special literary friend, Janet Adkins, for encouraging me to become a writer. Those emails you sent every morning kept me plugging along.

To C. Shea Lamone, author, for your guidance and for teaching me the three Ds of writing—desire, discipline and determination. You challenged me to be a better writer.

To Susan Elzy, author, for your reviews and patience as I wandered through revision after revision after revision....

To Joyce Maddox and Amy Moore of Warwick House Publishing, for your final editing and taking this story and turning it into a book for me. Another dream you made come true for me.

To the Martha Washington Inn, a favorite place I like to visit every year. Thanks for the inspiration that motivated me to write this book.

To a special Lil' Woman in my life, Jackie, my wife.
Thanks for your patience while I wrote this book
and nudging me on to be a better person.

CHAPTER 1

Trip to Abingdon

Putting his last set of clothes into the tote bag, Spencer looked around to see if he had forgotten to pack anything. Satisfied that he had everything needed for the trip, he put on his tan denim jacket and looked in the mirror to straighten his shirt collar. He ran his fingers through his brown, thinning hair so it wouldn't seem so frayed and rubbed his hand over his day-old beard, remembering he hadn't taken the time to shave. Clipping his cell phone onto his belt, he grabbed his stress-relief squeeze ball and tossed it into the air a couple of times before putting it into his bag. He zipped it closed and carried it down to the kitchen.

Almost forgetting, he left a message on the wall phone. "Hi, this is Spencer. I'll be gone through the weekend. If you need to contact me, call me on my cell or just leave a message and I'll contact you when I return. Thanks."

He went to the foyer and opened the door to leave. As he picked up his travel bags, he noticed that the sunlight beaming through the glass storm door was reflecting on the framed picture of Miriam, his wife. The sunlight made the dust visible on the picture, so he picked it up and wiped it clean with his coat sleeve. Staring at it for a moment, he thought, *Where did we go wrong? And why did we let it get to the point of separating?*

With a heavy sigh, he set the picture down and left. Before he got to his car, however, his neighbor yelled, "Morning, neighbor."

He saw Mr. Johnson, one of his elderly neighbors, walking his dog.

"Morning to you, Mr. Johnson. It's certainly a warm day for early November," he said, setting his luggage down to open the trunk on his Infinity Coupe. Mr. Johnson checked the weather report every morning and could give a weather forecast just as good as The Weather Channel.

"Yes, it is. The weather update this morning calls for warm and foggy days with cold and rainy nights for most of the week."

"Then I'm glad to be staying in the mountains instead of going to the beach. By the way, I'll be gone through the weekend. While you are out and about, would you mind keeping an eye on the condo for me?"

"Be glad to, Spencer, and I want to let you know that since the newspaper here quit publishing your articles and columns, it's not worth reading anymore. I canceled my subscription last week."

"Thank you for the compliment, Mr. Johnson. With advertising revenue down, they had to make some cuts somewhere. My columns, along with a couple of others, were canceled. I thought that after working with them for nineteen years my job was secure, but this recession is affecting everyone, I guess."

Mr. Johnson shook his head. "Well, I hope someone else will pick you up. You drive carefully, Spencer. I'll keep an eye on the place for you."

"Thank you, Mr. Johnson."

Spencer loaded his bags and closed the trunk.

A few miles down the road, his thoughts turned to Miriam, his wife of twenty-seven years. Their separation was going on four months now. He was trying to figure out why they had grown apart and if there was hope to save their marriage. After all, didn't they have the perfect American family? Both had careers, Miriam as an elementary school teacher and he as a writer for *The Charlottesville Observer*, writing articles on places of interest and their history.

Their children, Josh and Lynn, were pursuing careers and had marriages of their own. Having just recently paid off the mortgage on their Charlottesville home, Spencer and Miriam were at a time in life when they should be enjoying the fruits of their labors. But instead, it was obvious, they had drifted apart.

Maybe it was the conversations that turned quieter, suggestions that often became debates, or that patience was no longer a virtue they sought. Why had they let the passion they once had for each other subside? Was it the extra travel he found himself doing every week for his job to find bigger and better projects to write about or his more frequent trips to the club for golf or conversation with friends? Besides, wasn't Miriam always involved in community projects, charity work, or running to help some friend who was struggling with a midlife crisis? It had gotten to the point that they just went through the motions to be together and tolerate each other. Something had to give, and separating until each could figure out what they wanted had seemed to be the right thing to do. Agreeing to let Miriam stay in their home, Spencer moved into a condo he had leased just outside of Charlottesville.

After the separation, though, Spencer realized that he was even more unhappy and discontented than when he was living with Miriam. His social life crashed, he had no desire to be around crowds, and he began to avoid all unnecessary travel. Every morning when he woke up and every night when he went to bed, Miriam was the first and last thought on his mind. It seemed like their separation was just too easy to do. There were no arguments or fighting over assets or money. It was almost as if both of them were still trying to look after the interest of the other. He began to wonder if separating was the right thing to do, but he also knew that he would never want to go back to the same stale relationship.

Now living alone, Spencer found himself longing to be back with the girl he had fallen in love with almost thirty years ago. He had thought long and hard about talking to Miriam to see if there was a chance to make their marriage work, then things had gotten worse. Two months after the separation, he lost his job. He decided that before they could have a chance to work things out, he first needed to find employment and get his career secure. And he didn't know what Miriam's thoughts were.

As he turned right onto 64 West, his cell phone rang. The name of Elaine Wampler, his friend and agent, appeared on the screen.

"Hello, Elaine," he answered.

"Hello, Spencer. I called you at home and heard your message, so I knew you were on your way. I just wanted to check to see if I need to take care of anything for you while you're away."

"No, everything's fine. I've just turned onto 64 West and will be on 81 South heading to Abingdon in a minute."

"Great. I have a suite reserved for you. I've also arranged for an acquaintance to meet with you today at four o'clock, if that's all right. Her name is Bernice Ferguson. She's a retired school-teacher and has written several articles on history in southwest Virginia, especially Abingdon. I thought maybe she could give you some ideas to write about or perhaps do some research for you."

Spencer hesitated. "Thanks for the effort, Elaine. I know you have a lot of faith in my writing. But with the problems Miriam and I've had over the last two years, and now the separation, along with losing my job, I'm not sure I'm in a frame of mind to write anything right now."

"I understand what you're saying, Spencer. But look at the novel you wrote three years ago. It's selling better now than when you first published it. I know it's not on a best seller list, but I think if you publish another one it'll help get your work established. Then your writing will find a following. It's all about being discovered, and you're a gifted writer. I want to see you succeed."

Spencer sighed. "I'll try to get something started. I just don't know where to begin. Maybe you're right. A few days at this inn in Abingdon will make a difference. Maybe I can find something interesting for a good book." He paused to change lanes. "And

4

maybe find a distraction to get my mind off all of my problems for a while."

"I have confidence in you, Spencer. I'll be in Abingdon visiting my sister on Saturday. Maybe we can connect and have brunch before you start back home."

"That would be good. And, Elaine, thanks for believing in me."

He could almost hear her smile.

"I always have and always will. Drive carefully and watch your speed on 81. You know the state police will be out with radar. Call me if I can help with anything."

"I will, and thanks for your friendship and help. Bye now."

Elaine worked for a small publishing company as an agent for a lot of local writers of short stories, novels, and articles of interest. Spencer had met Elaine at The Virginia Book Festival in Charlottesville while she was doing a seminar on how to get published the first time. He had shown her a historical novel he had written. She convinced him to publish it and was able to get a contract for him. It got him noticed, but not accepted by the big publishing companies yet. He had wanted to write another book, but with all the travel his job demanded and the problems he and Miriam experienced over the last two years, he just hadn't had the inspiration.

Being the friend she was, however, Elaine knew he was out of work and needed something on which to focus. To encourage him to write again, her company was picking up the tab on his visit to the inn at Abingdon, hoping he would find some history there that would inspire him to write again.

As he turned onto US 81 South, Spencer continued to think about his life and marriage. He had gone to college at UVA in Charlottesville where he graduated with a degree in literature and arts. While in school, he took a couple of classes in creative writing and wrote several articles, one of which the local newspaper published. Upon graduation, he got a job offer from the newspaper. The excitement of pursuing his destiny through his own newspaper column was far more appealing than teaching in a classroom, so he accepted.

Two years later, at a Chamber of Commerce Business after Hours meeting hosted by the local board of education, he met Miriam. She caught his attention when they entered the room together during the social hour. She was a petite girl with wavy brown hair, light hazel eyes, and a beautiful smile. Several times during the evening they caught each other's glances.

Spencer remembered stepping up to the bar and asking for a glass of wine. While waiting, he glanced across the room to find this beautiful lady smiling back at him. That did it. He began making his way across the room to formally introduce himself.

Trying to casually make his way over to her, he was stopped numerous times by people who wanted to talk about some of his articles. Not wanting to be rude, but also wanting to get across the room, Spencer continued to move along and cut their conversations short when possible. Step after step, person after person, he struggled to stay focused on the conversations as he moved toward the other side of the room. Finally making it, he turned to greet her, but she was gone. A little frustrated, he turned around and was pleased to find her standing behind him, smiling, and holding two glasses of wine.

"I went to the bar, and the bartender said you walked away before getting your glass of wine. I told him that I might have been the cause of it, so here it is," she said.

Spencer laughed and said, "You're probably right. It took me ten minutes to walk forty feet across here with so many people wanting to talk."

"I can see that you're popular." She handed him the glass of wine and extended her hand. "By the way, my name is Miriam. I'm speaking to the business community tonight about co-oping with the local educators on the Merits of Graduation Program for our school kids."

Still holding her hand, he said, "My name is Spencer Aubreys. I'm a writer for one of the local papers."

"Yes, I've read your articles. Now I know why you're so much in demand."

"I'm just trying to make a living. I'm looking forward to your presentation."

She stared down at her glass, avoiding his eyes, smiling nervously, "Actually, I'm a little nervous. This is different from a classroom of kids, you know."

"No, not really, we're just a little naughtier, I'm sure."

They continued to talk and laugh until it was time for Miriam to speak.

Spencer was so attracted to her that he couldn't take his eyes off her all evening. Two days after the Chamber meeting, he called and asked her out. Two years later they were married.

Checking the speedometer, Spencer passed the Wytheville exit. Another call came in on his cell phone. When he saw Miriam's number, he took a deep breath in anticipation.

"Hello, Miriam," he said, trying to conceal the nervousness in his voice.

"Hi, Spencer, I called and got your message at home. Where are you going, a potential job interview?"

"I wish. Elaine convinced me to go down and spend a few days at an inn in Abingdon. She wants me to do some research, hoping I'll come up with a good idea for a second book."

"Well, at least it'll keep your mind off not working."

"Believe me, I would rather be working," he said with a laugh.

"Do you need some extra money? We could withdraw something from our savings." She sounded concerned.

"No, I'm fine for now. I'm trying not to spend any more than I need to. I just don't know when I'll find work. I'm fifty years old, and all I've done is write for a newspaper. Everyone is downsizing until the recession is over, so it could be who knows how long before I find work again."

"Well, you know the money is there if you need it. We both have to agree to release it, but I'd be glad to."

"I know," he exhaled. "Life just gets more complicated, doesn't it?"

She agreed, then said, "The reason I called is that Josh and Lynn both want to come in for Thanksgiving. Can you join us, or do you have other plans?"

"No, I don't have other plans. Of course I want to see them." He swallowed hard. "How are they dealing with our separation?"

"They're both very sad and upset about it." She paused. "You need to call them more often."

"Yes, I know," he said reluctantly, knowing she was right.

There was a long pause before she spoke again. "Spencer, there's something I need to let you know. There is someone who's been asking me out, and I'm thinking about taking him up on the offer. What do you think?"

Catching his breath, he breathed out slowly before answering. "I thought we both agreed that we would not question each other's personal life once we separated."

"I know it's in the agreement, but..."

Irritation, or was it jealousy, rising sharply within him, he interrupted, "Well, Miriam, I'm not your keeper. You have to decide what you want to do."

It was her turn to raise her voice.

"Look, I was just trying to be nice since you're dealing with our separation and now losing your job. I know you're already on edge and I didn't want to put you on the spot if someone told you they saw me out with someone else."

"Miriam, you do what you feel like you need to do." Spencer closed the subject.

"Spencer, I'm sorry I called. Goodbye!" Click.

Spencer pressed the off button, and then threw the phone down. *Dammit! Why did I pick an argument with her? It always ends this way.*

He wasn't even sure what they had argued about, as usual. It was just such a surprise to hear that she might be going out with someone. Taking a deep breath, he tried to calm himself. *Maybe she wanted me to say no, or maybe she's like me since we separated— even more confused and unhappy. I can't ask her to let me come home now. With no job, she would think I was coming home out of desperation for her to support me. I have to find a way to work through this, for me and for her. I know I still love her. But does she still love me?*

He considered that question for a while, and then concluded. *Maybe not, if she's thinking about dating.*

Spencer read the road sign as he drove by the town of Marion, only thirty miles away from Abingdon. Forcing himself to focus, his thoughts turned back to his trip and visit to the Inn at Abingdon.

CHAPTER 2
A Guest in Abingdon

A light drizzle began to fall as Spencer took Exit 17 off I-81 into Abingdon. The thickening fog was rolling in and he was glad he would not be driving later in the day. While sitting at a traffic light, he looked at his Googled directions and saw that turning right at the second light onto Main Street, only a few hundred feet ahead, would put him at his destination.

He parked up on the knoll of the unloading zone where a large water fountain stood surrounded by landscaped shrubs and bushes now covered with the last of fall's discarded leaves. To his right, a large porch stretched across the front of the Inn. A white wooden rail reached from end to end, and various flags hung over the porch that had several chairs for lounging.

An older, gray-haired gentleman dressed in a gray uniform greeted him at the door.

"Good evening, sir. My name is Allen. Welcome to the Inn. Will you be staying with us?"

"Yes, I am." He nodded as Allen reached for the door.

"Have you stayed with us before?" Allen asked.

Shaking his head, Spencer said, "No, this is my first time."

"Our receptionist, Julia, is across the foyer to your right," he pointed. "She will assist you with check-in. I'll wait here to help you with your bags."

"Thank you."

Spencer stepped inside where the focal point of the lobby foyer was a round, wooden antique table with a marble top that held a large vase of multi-colored flowers. An elaborate chandelier above the table enhanced their beauty. Plush chairs and a sofa were placed strategically throughout the room. The wooden plank floor creaked and popped under his feet as he made his way to the receptionist counter.

"Good evening," he greeted the receptionist. "I'm Spencer Aubreys. I should have a room reserved through Saturday."

"Yes, Mr. Aubreys, we're expecting you. My name is Julia, and I'm one of the day receptionists." Thumbing through her files, the middle-aged, attractive brunette pulled his information. "Your reservation includes breakfast every morning as well as a hundred dollar gift voucher that can be used at the spa or in the dining room."

"I didn't know I was getting the royal treatment. I didn't book the reservation," he said with a smile.

"Someone must think a lot of you." She smiled back and handed him a key.

"Yes, she's been a real friend lately."

"Your room is on the third floor. Our elevator goes up to the second floor, and then you'll have a flight of stairs to get to your room. Allen, our bellhop, will get your bags to the room, which is number 300. Here's a flyer that shows scheduled events throughout the week, and we have tea time from 4 to 6 daily in this room."

Taking the flyer, he glanced over to where she pointed. "That sounds great."

"Please let us know what we can do to make your stay with us pleasant and memorable." She smiled as she folded her arms and leaned on the counter.

"Certainly, Julia. I'm looking forward to my stay here. I'm going to run and get parked before the rain gets worse."

"Yes, it's supposed to get colder and rain more tonight. In fact, it's going to be like this for the next four days with warm days, cool nights, and lots of rain."

Back outside, Allen stood beside Spencer's car and greeted him again.

"Mr. Aubreys, again welcome to the Inn. I'll get your bags to your room while you park."

"Thank you, I'll be right in."

A few minutes later, he met Allen in his room. Seeing his bags had made it safely, he handed him a tip.

"Mr. Aubreys, I have placed a bottle of champagne on ice for you, compliments of the Inn. Is there more I can do for you?"

He glanced around the room. "No, everything is fine."

"Please call down to the receptionist if you need me. We want to make your stay enjoyable."

As Spencer explored the room, he was surprised at the elegant but older style furnishings and colorful décor as if it were a setting from another time and place. An obvious effort had been made to recreate the 1800s.

The antique poster bed sat so high that Spencer was glad he had a step stool to get on it. The flowered wallpaper, fabric on the sofa and chairs, and antique furniture all added warm ambiance to a room that still had its original wooden floor, covered now by a luxurious antique designer rug.

A small chess table by the window caught his eye. Immediately getting his satchel, he laid out his laptop, pens, and writing pads. Then he proceeded to unpack his clothing since he would be there for the next five days.

At four o'clock, almost time to meet Bernice, he locked the door behind him and went down to the lobby where he poured himself a cup of hot cider from the server. After taking a seat on the sofa, he saw a lady dressed in black and white with a black cape around her shoulders enter the room.

She greeted Julia, and then asked, "Do we have any guests wanting to do the ghost tour this evening?"

"No, no one signed up," Julia replied, "unless Mr. Aubreys, our guest here, would like to do it." She gestured toward Spencer.

The lady in the cape turned to Spencer. "Good evening, my name is Madame Maria. Would you like to join me on the ghost tour and history lesson this evening? I promise to make it chilling." She spoke in a low, mysterious voice.

"Sounds interesting, but I'm meeting someone here in a few minutes." He smiled and opened his palm out. "Besides, I wouldn't want to get any spirits up on my account. It might make them mad."

She returned his laugh and gesture. "Well, we've been known to have a few encounters with them here. However, no one has ever been hurt, maybe just spent a restless night while here."

"Then that's a good reason for me to leave them alone. Maybe if I let them rest in peace, they will return the favor."

"Well, if you change your mind, I'll be back here Friday evening around six o'clock." She walked away.

Spencer leaned forward on the sofa. "Julia, are there many people here now?"

"No, we've been slow, especially during the weekdays. The economy has taken a toll on our business."

"I think everyone has been affected in some way," he replied. "It's most likely going to take a couple of years before we see much improvement. And just think, we paid a bunch of lawyers in Washington big salaries over the past two decades to get us in this fix."

She leaned forward, her elbows on the counter. "What kind of work do you do, Mr. Aubreys?"

"I'm kind of unemployed right now. I hope to do some writing while I'm here, though."

Resting her chin on a fist, she raised an eyebrow. "That's interesting. What do you write?"

"Mostly historical fiction. A lady who's going to brief me on some of the history of Abingdon is meeting me here."

The door opened, and Spencer turned to see a tall white-haired lady entering the room. She was dressed in a gray skirt, white blouse and a gray jacket. Brushing the rain off and standing her umbrella in the corner, she said, "Evening, Julia, I'm here to meet a Spencer Aubreys. Has he checked in yet?"

Julia pointed to Spencer. "Yes, there he is on the sofa."

She turned toward him and said. "I apologize. I didn't see you sitting there. I'm Bernice Ferguson, Elaine's friend."

"That's quite all right." Spencer stood up. "Thanks for coming out in this nasty weather."

"No problem, I live about five minutes from here. Elaine's sister is my neighbor. They are both wonderful ladies."

"I only know Elaine, and yes, I have to agree." He gestured toward the server, "Would you care for a beverage, maybe tea or cider? Then we can go to the library behind us and talk or go to the room across the foyer."

"Let's go across the foyer. It may be less noisy."

After filling their cups with cider, they headed for the foyer. Bernice glanced back and said before leaving, "Julia, give me a call. Maybe we can do lunch one day when you're not working."

"That's a good idea. We can get caught up on what's happened in Abingdon. You two enjoy the evening."

In the room, they sat in plush comfortable chairs. Bernice leaned to one side and rested an arm on the chair's arm. "Elaine said that you wrote a book about three years ago and you want to start another one." She sipped her cider.

Spencer crossed his legs and laid his notepad on his lap. "I'm attempting to start one."

"What period of Abingdon's history would you like to know about?"

"Can we start with this inn?"

"Excellent choice." She sat her cup of cider down on a small table beside her and began. "This inn was originally built as a private home in the early 1800s. The family later left and sold it to be a girls' boarding school. During the Civil War, it became a hospital for wounded soldiers, both Union and Confederate. There are lots of stories about romances kindled, hearts broken, and even tragedy when a lot of the young girls stayed to help with the wounded during the war." She paused as Spencer scribbled notes and then continued.

"Abingdon was a major supply route for supplies coming up from the south to the Confederates during the Civil War. Supplies were brought up by rail, then moved north by wagon, since the Union sabotaged most of the rails in northern Virginia. Abingdon had its own militia, but they had to work discreetly since the Union stayed close to see if they could catch anyone moving supplies. A lot of the militia's movement in and out of Abingdon was done in a network of underground tunnels that are still beneath the city today, but closed off to the public. The town of Abingdon was always under the threat of being burned down by the Union, and part of it eventually was."

Spencer flipped his page over, and she took the chance to sip some more cider.

"After the war, it once again became a boarding school for girls until it was closed in the early 1900s. Eventually, investors bought it and refurbished it to become one of Virginia's most favorite inns."

Glancing around, Spencer said, "They've done a great job preserving the history within these walls—the leather and fabric-covered antique chairs, the original wooden floors and look at that nineteenth century grandfather clock. You can't help but think you're in another time and place once you come inside."

Nodding her head, she agreed, then asked, "What are some of the other places or events in history you'd like to talk about?"

"You just pick your favorite time and place, and I'll listen."

For an hour, Bernice continued to bring Abingdon to life in times long past. Finally, about five-thirty, they agreed that he had absorbed all the information he could for one day.

Bernice stood to leave. "Here's my card. Call me if you have questions, or if you would like to chat again. I promise if I don't have answers to your questions, I'll find someone who does."

They shook hands. "Thank you, Bernice, you've been so kind."

After she left, Spencer went upstairs to his room and stood in front of the window, stretching. The rain had stopped, but there was now a heavy fog developing all around.

He sat at the table, looking over his notes, and contemplated what he might start writing about. Finally, he realized he didn't have a clue. Picking up his squeeze ball, he sat back and gazed out the window into the evening as darkness began to drown out daylight.

His thoughts drifted back to the conversation he and Miriam had earlier. He had to admit that he missed her as he reflected back to when their time together was good. He remembered the weekend getaways at bed-and-breakfast inns they had visited, the laughter and fun of raising their children, and the plans they made for retirement years that were all but lost now. As the light in his room grew dimmer, the question of when their love started falling apart was heavy on his mind. *Maybe we both just got too busy and lost our priorities. Would she believe me if I called and told her I wanted to come back, or would she think I was desperate because I am unemployed?* Leaning forward, he rested his head in his hands, elbows on the table, but no answers came, even though he knew he eventually had to work through it somehow.

Suddenly, he heard popping and creaking caused by someone walking on the wooden floor outside his room. His door flew open, and a draft of cold air blew into the room. Thinking he did not close the door tightly when entering, he walked over and looked outside to see who had come up to the third floor. Seeing no one, however, he closed the door. But the chill lingered in the room.

Startled out of his reverie, he decided to put on his jacket for a walk around the Inn since it was still early evening.

Maybe a walk outside will clear my mind, and I will think of something to write about. It's better than sitting here feeling sorry for myself, he thought as he continued downstairs to the lower floor hallway.

CHAPTER 3

The Visit

Walking down the main hallway, Spencer admired the beautifully carpeted floors, the wallpaper, and especially the many glistening chandeliers hanging from high ceilings. He passed a café to his right, smelling freshly brewed coffee, then came to a second hallway that added another wing to the Inn, down yet another set of steps by the spa entrance and out the back door. A few more steps took him to a rock patio where he noticed a small secluded seating area to his left and to his right a large whirlpool tub encircled by rocks and flowering shrubs with a seating area beside it. A rock sidewalk wound down and around the pool area. Strolling down to the back lower lot, he spied a gazebo and walked over to it for a closer look.

As he looked through the thickening fog at the well-groomed landscape and mulched beds around him, Spencer thought, *How did I ever miss the opportunity to write about this inn? If I ever get hired to write a newspaper column again, this is one of the first places I will write about. With all the history and its antique furnishings and its modern-day amenities, it would be an exciting place to write about.*

Looking across the lot toward the railroad tracks, Spencer noticed a girl standing to his right about twenty feet away on the lower corner lot. She wore a pale-blue dress that dropped to the ground. Her long hair draped across her shoulders and fell loosely onto her back. Curious about her being out there alone, Spencer decided to speak to her.

"Good evening, ma'am."

Obviously startled, she jumped at his words. When she turned toward him and looked, he could see fear in her eyes.

Spencer apologized, "I didn't mean to startle you. I'm staying here at the Inn and just came out to look around and get a breath of fresh air before it gets dark."

She paused and then replied, "Yes, I had to come out also and get away for a spell. So much is going on, so many people are hurting."

A light drizzle began to fall. "Look," Spencer said, "it's starting to rain again. You'd better come in or you're going to get wet."

"I suppose you're right."

She began walking toward the gazebo. Spencer walked out to help her step across the mulched landscaping in her path. As she got closer, her thin, small frame and radiant auburn hair almost illuminated the fog and darkness that surrounded her.

He extended his hand to help her across the mulch, and she carefully lifted her dress. She took a long step to get across, lost her balance and fell against him. Helping her steady herself, he was close enough that when she looked up he saw her soft, blue eyes and velvet-smooth complexion and decided she was no more than fifteen or sixteen years old.

She felt cold against him, so he asked, "Are you okay?"

Pulling her hand away, she answered, "I'm fine, thank you."

"Here, take my coat." He removed his coat and wrapped it around her shoulders. "This should keep you warm until we get back inside."

Stepping into the gazebo to get out of the drizzling rain, he said, "My name is Spencer. What's yours?"

"Katherine...Katherine..." She hesitated. "Katherine Broadwater, but not for long. When Sam comes home from the war, my name will change." She spoke softly, not meeting his eyes.

Assuming that meant they would be married, Spencer said, "Then I guess congratulations are in order. When will he be coming home?"

"Most any day now. I was afraid for him to return to the war, since he had been wounded and almost died. But he said he

18

had to see the war finished before he could settle down and have peace."

"He must be a true hero." Spencer thought of similar stories of other young men who also went back to fight in Iraq or Afghanistan.

"I'm just tired of the fighting and killing that happens every day. Everyone is frightened, trying not to take sides and living in fear every day."

Spencer, not sure where the conversation was going, realized the rain was coming down faster, and said, "Let's make our way back up to the Inn. It's getting dark. We don't need to get caught in a downpour." He took his coat and pulled it tight around her shoulders.

Walking side by side up the rock sidewalk, Spencer became even more curious and asked, "Where are you from?"

"A place called Copper Creek, about a day's ride west of here. I was going to school, but once the war got here, most of us girls stayed and volunteered to help take care of the wounded. That's how I met Sam."

As they reached the patio, Spencer tried to put into perspective what Katherine had said. Her talk about the war and staying to care for the wounded didn't make a lot of sense. He was unaware of any hospital in this area that cared for wounded veterans.

Katherine stopped, reached and picked a flower from a bush beside the patio. She rubbed each pink petal between her finger tips as if touching a flower for the first time. Then she lifted it, smelling the blossom, and her eyes turned to Spencer. Admiring the beauty of this young girl speaking with a southern accent that he had never heard before, Spencer felt his writer's curiosity being aroused.

Wanting to continue the conversation to learn more and get Katherine out of the cold, he suggested, "Why don't we go inside and have a coffee?"

"Yes, I suppose I need to go in. I'm sure my help is needed."

He stepped onto the patio, extended his hand to help Katherine up and then turned toward the steps to the Inn where he discovered Allen standing.

As Spencer approached him, Allen turned and said, "Oh, Mr. Aubreys, I have a message for you from the front desk. Someone by the name of Miriam called and said she tried calling you on your cell phone but couldn't get you. She said if we saw you to relay the message. No emergency, though."

"Sure, I'll call her. Thank you."

"You dropped your coat behind you." Allen pointed to the patio floor.

Spencer turned and found his coat lying on the patio deck. Reaching for it, he saw lying on top of it the flower Katherine had picked. He gathered up his coat and then looked out into the darkness, but saw only droplets of rain reflecting the outside lights of the Inn.

He called her name, "Katherine! Katherine!"

"Mr. Aubreys, can I help?" Spencer heard Allen say behind him. He turned to see a seemingly confused Allen.

"Yes, I was talking to a young girl named Katherine. She was right behind me wearing my jacket. Now she's gone. She was dressed in a long, pale-blue dress and had long, auburn hair. Didn't you see her?"

"No, I didn't even see you until I heard you start up the steps."

Spencer brushed the water from his coat. "Does she work here?"

"No, I can't think of anyone named Katherine or who even fits that description that works here."

It was Spencer's turn to look confused. "I can't believe she just walked off."

"Maybe she's one of the actresses who walked over from the theater to take a break. I see them over here once in awhile," Allen said.

"Maybe so," Spencer conceded, as he followed Allen back into the Inn. *Perhaps that's why she talks with an accent. What she said about the war going on and her life didn't make a lot of sense. Hope I can see her again. She seems like an interesting person.*

Inside his room a few minutes later, Spencer lit the gas logs in the fireplace. Still holding the flower Katherine had picked, he went to the room bar, drew water in a glass, placed the stem of the flower in it, and then set it on the corner of the table by the window.

Remembering he needed to call Miriam, he retrieved his phone from the bedroom, sat at the desk by the window and dialed.

She answered, "Hello, Spencer. Thanks for calling. I just wanted to make sure you made it to Abingdon okay." She paused. "Also, I want to apologize for hanging up earlier."

"I made it fine. Thanks for calling." He hesitated. "I don't blame you for hanging up on me. What I said wasn't nice. It's just that I'm on edge and have a lot on my mind. I'll figure it out eventually, though."

"Spencer, I want you to know I understand what you're going through. Our separation, and now losing your job, has to be stressful. But I want to help in some way if you'll let me." Her voice trailed off.

"Thank you, Miriam. I'll let you know," he said defensively, drawing a deep breath.

She changed the subject. "How do you like the Inn?"

"It's a beautiful place. You would approve of it. Reminds me of some of the bed-and breakfast-inns we used to visit, just much larger. There's hardly anyone here this week." Picking up the squeeze ball, he mashed it in his hand.

"Have you found anything interesting to write about?"

"Actually, I have, or I think so. I was just outside and met a young girl. She had a really different southern accent and kind of a strange story to tell."

"What kind of strange story?"

"I'm not sure. Something about her and a boy named Sam who's coming home from the war and they are planning to get married." He laid the squeeze ball down and picked up the glass with the flower.

"Why do you think that's strange?"

"I don't know. It's something about how she was dressed in what looked like an old-fashioned dress and spoke with a southern Appalachian accent that sounded so different. Maybe it's just my writer's curiosity kicking in. You know, after all, I did come down to write."

"Will you see her again?"

"I'm not sure. She kind of left suddenly when Allen, the bellhop, caught my attention to tell me you'd called. He said that she was probably an actress who was taking a break from the theater beside the Inn."

"If a story is there, I'm sure you will find it."

"I definitely could use a distraction now. No job..." He hesitated..."and trying to figure us out." He picked up his stress ball again.

"We'll figure it out. You just need to relax and not get so stressed out over everything."

"Miriam, that's easy for you to say. Your life hasn't completely fallen apart like mine has." He took a deep breath and squeezed the ball.

She replied with agitation in her voice. "Do you think my life is better since we've separated? Do you think I'm living in a world of bliss now?"

"Miriam, I didn't say that."

"Spencer, the last thing I intended to do was call you to start a fight. Why do we always end up fighting when we talk?"

"Miriam, I'm sorry. Forget that I mentioned it." He slumped back into his chair.

"Good night, Spencer." Click.

It happened again. He put his face in his hands and tried to figure out why their conversations were always so defensive.

Then looking out the window, he gazed down on the street where glaring lights from the street posts shattered the darkness. A downpour of rain blew against the windowpanes, dripping to the porch.

Glancing back at the fire and then at the flower on the desk, he decided to try to write. He turned on his laptop and began. Not sure where he was going with a story, he started thinking about Katherine and the conversation they had earlier. He hoped to see her again, so maybe she could give him more to write about. Or maybe even be a character for him to use in a story. After all, she was an interesting person with whom to talk.

CHAPTER 4

The Meeting

At the sound of unfamiliar voices, Spencer turned over in bed. Opening his eyes, he realized he wasn't at home in his own bed, and the voices were coming from outside the Inn. After a couple of stretches, he slowly sat up in bed. There was a chill in the room, so he lit the gas logs in the fireplace and stood for a moment letting the flames warm him.

He reflected back to the night before when he had stayed up until midnight trying to get a story started for his book. His first attempts were to build a story around Katherine, the young girl he had encountered earlier, knowing that whatever he wrote, it would be fiction. Still very curious about who she was and about her life's story, Spencer had become antsy. *I have to find her, and maybe she'll give me an interview. Maybe I can use her as a character. After all, her accent, dress, and southern charm would help bring a story to life.*

By midnight, exhausted from thinking about Katherine and trying to solve her identity, then Miriam and their earlier conversations, he hadn't been able to find sleep. In fact, since their separation and worrying about his job loss, sleep was something that eluded his tired and busy mind most of the time.

After showering, in hopes of waking up more, he stepped to the vanity to shave. Lathering his two-day old bearded face, he reached into his bag for a razor that wasn't there. *So much for shaving today.* Washing the lather from his face, he decided it would be a good week not to shave. Every year around Thanksgiving, he always quit shaving for a couple of weeks anyway. He chuckled at the memory—

Miriam always liked him unshaven for the first week, but after that he would always find his razor lying on his sink basin. It was her way of saying it was time to shave.

Out of habit, he pulled the blanket and bedspread up. If there was one thing Miriam had gotten him into the habit of doing, it was to always clean up, pick up, or straighten up what needed to be done around the house. He never minded, since she worked full-time, and he felt it was only fair to help with the housework.

Spencer went to the dining room for breakfast and took a seat. A young, petite lady wearing an apron stepped up and said, "Good morning, can I start you off with juice or coffee?"

"Yes, let's make the juice an orange, grapefruit combo and coffee. I can give you my breakfast order now also."

"Sure, go ahead." She poured the coffee.

"I want the sweet potato pancakes, bowl of fruit, and a side of bacon."

"Great choice," she said. She sat the coffee pot down and smiled. "I'll have your food to you in a moment."

As Spencer sat and waited, he thought about all the bed-and-breakfast inns he and Miriam had visited during their twenty-seven years of marriage. The walls in their den were full of prints of many they had stayed in. There had been at least twenty. He was sure Mariam would like this one.

After breakfast, Spencer decided to learn his way around town and stopped at the front desk on his way out.

"Good morning, Julia." He smiled and leaned on the counter.

"Good morning, Mr. Aubreys," she replied, holding a stack of papers she was filing. "Do you have a big day planned?"

"No, not really. I'm thinking about finding the trail around here that everyone talks about."

"Oh, yes," she gestured toward the outside. "The Creeper Trail. You'll certainly enjoy it."

"That's it. How do I get to it?"

She pointed to her right. "Leave the Inn, take a right at the corner and go to the end of the block across the railroad tracks.

The trail starts to your left. It might be a little wet right now because of the rain last night. It should be dried off by this afternoon, though."

"Then I'll wait. What time does the theater open?"

She glanced at her watch, and answered, "It opens at ten. But shows don't start until seven. If you like, we would be glad to get tickets for you."

Spencer held up his hand. "No, I want to go over and see if I can find out about a young lady I met here last night."

Her eyebrows rose. "Does she work there?"

"I'm not sure. She was a young lady by the name of Katherine Broadwater. She wore what looked like an old-fashioned dress and had a very different accent. She was telling me about herself, and I thought about interviewing her more to possibly write a story around her. I think she's an actress."

"That could be a good place to find her then."

He patted the counter as an end to the conversation. "Thanks for the information, Julia."

She turned back to her filing. "Certainly, Mr. Aubreys. You have a great day."

Spencer walked across the street and made his way to the theater. The air was warm and humid, and a thick fog lingered. He entered through the heavy glass doors and looked around for a moment at wall posters of shows, past and present, then stepped up to the counter to speak to the clerk.

"Excuse me, but I'm looking for someone who may be an actress here."

"And who might that be?" A tall gray-haired man posed the question as he leaned forward on the counter with both hands.

"Her name is Katherine Broadwater," Spencer said, rubbing his chin in anticipation of the answer he would get.

The man shook his head. "I'm sorry, but we don't have anyone with that name working here." His eyes narrowed. "Did she say she worked here?"

"No, she didn't. I just thought that maybe she was an actress. Sorry, it's my mistake."

"That's quite all right."

Spencer left the theater and walked back across the street and up a couple of blocks on Main Street, admiring the old block and brick buildings. Many had signs showing the dates of construction and a brief history and information on them. He came upon a rock building called "The Tavern," built in 1779, which was first used as a lodge for stagecoach travelers, but today as a restaurant for white tablecloth dining.

Spencer returned to the Inn, grabbed his laptop and went back out to the gazebo.

He began typing notes describing the surrounding landscape and the dense fog that continued to linger. Instinctively, he felt the presence of someone watching him. At first glance he saw no one. Then he looked toward the railroad tracks and saw Katherine looking at him from the corner of the lot.

Excited to see her, he walked from the gazebo and called her name.

"Katherine…Katherine."

She stared back but didn't speak.

"It's me—Spencer. Remember we met last night?"

Finally, she nodded and moved toward him.

Spencer thought it was strange that she wore the same pale-blue dress and stood in the exact same spot where he saw her last night. Once again, he reached to help her step across the mulch.

"I was hoping to see you again. You left so suddenly last night."

"Yes, I had so much to do for so many that I had to go back in and work."

"What kind of work do you do?"

"I help Rosa with the cooking and chores and tend to the wounded." She glanced up toward the Inn.

Spencer crossed his arms and leaned against a gazebo column before asking, "Where do you work?"

Again, she glanced up toward the Inn and replied, "Here at the hospital."

Not fully understanding, Spencer thought it best to stop asking her questions, since he did not want to make her uncomfortable and scare her off. For some reason, she fascinated him and captivated his curiosity. So much so that he was determined to get her to open up about herself so he could learn more about her. He decided to try another approach.

"I'm a writer," he said. "Would you share your life's story with me? Just tell me about the things you are comfortable with. I'm hoping that some of what you tell me could be used in my next book."

She stared at him with confusion on her face and said, "I don't understand."

"Let's sit under the gazebo, and I'll help you get started." He pointed to a seat.

Seated on the opposite bench with his laptop open, Spencer began to question Katherine. "Tell me about yourself. Tell me about your family."

Katherine stared into space for a moment as if trying to remember, looked back and began.

"My family lives on a farm west of here near a ridge called Copper Creek. The land is rocky and hilly, except for the spot where we raise our fresh vegetables. During the droughts, all of us young ones carry water from the creek to water the crop. Sometimes it takes most of the day to do it." She spoke slowly, making it easy for Spencer to keep up.

"Mama always puts away as much food as she can, since we are nine mouths to feed—Mama, Papa, my brothers, sisters and me. Papa often goes to Saltville to work in the salt mines after summer or helps cut trestles for the railroad to get money to buy things we can't raise on the land. Thomas and Noel, my older brothers, keep the place up until Papa returns.

"When I turned fourteen, Mama wanted me to get a good learning so she brought me here to the boarding school. I have to work to help pay my way, but Mama said I need proper schooling so I could someday meet and marry a well-to-do gentleman who will take care of me and give me a better life.

"I've been here for nearly a year and a half now. Things just aren't the same since the fighting started, though. Everyone is scared to take sides, and there are so many men and boys dying or getting hurt. Our school is a hospital now. Mama wanted me to come home, but a lot of us girls are staying to help take care of the sick and wounded. It scares me trying to care for both sides. We have to keep them apart so they won't kill each other. I'll be glad when this war is over and Sam can come home. He promised he would come back to me."

Spencer, intrigued, gave her all of his attention. He listened closely and realized that she was talking about another time and place. Although he didn't understand what she was talking about or where she was going with this story, he decided to listen and see where the story went.

Curiosity was getting the best of him, even as he sat thinking. *Katherine is obviously not from here. She is either a darn good actress or one great story teller. I guess the only way I'm going to find out who this girl is and why she's telling me this story is to sit and listen. After all, I came here to write, didn't I?*

Longing to learn more, he continued to question her.

"Tell me about the hospital and about Sam. How did you meet?"

Katherine looked up toward the Inn for a moment, then back down at Spencer. With her small hands clasped together in her lap and her eyes sparkling, she began to speak with quiet enthusiasm.

CHAPTER 5

The Story

It was another hot August evening in Abingdon as Rosa hummed, "Swing Low Swing Chariot," while folding the sheets she had just pulled from the clothesline. Standing in front of the clothes basket on the back porch of the boarding school that was now a hospital, a breeze gave relief from the summer heat. The tragedy and hardships Abingdon recently had to endure because of the War Between the States seemed far away.

A house servant to a wealthy family most of her life, Rosa and Thomas, her husband, were given their freedom by Mr. Duke just as the war began a couple years before. Mr. Duke had offered to send them up north away from all the fighting and unrest the war was causing. But they had wanted to stay in Abingdon since it was the only home they had ever known. With a small house they could call their home, and now getting paid for the work they did, they were much better off than most black folks.

Being the bubbly person she was, Rosa was everyone's friend, especially with all the young girls who attended the boarding school. Often the girls would come to Rosa and share matters they would not talk about to anyone else. Many called her "Mama Rosa," especially when she was quick to give the girls advice.

Katherine walked up on the back porch with a basket of eggs she had collected from the hen house.

Rosa asked, "Can ya help me fold these linens while I goes hang up another load to dry? Can't believe we goes through all these beddings the way we does. All the bleedin' goin' on, wonder anybody still livin'."

"Yes, Rosa, I'll be glad to." Katherine began folding the sheets and cloths heaped up in front of her.

"I'll take the washin' and hang'em fo ya," Thomas said, as he walked out onto the porch. "I done finish bringin' fresh water in so's I got me some time to hep ya."

She handed him a basket of linens. "When ya finishes, bring me a couple buckets of them taters out of de ground cellar so's we can start peelin' 'em fo supper."

"Sho will," Thomas agreed as he stepped away with a basket of wet linens.

Thomas, being a tall, stout man, took care of harvesting the gardens, cutting the firewood, tending to the farm animals and other outside chores. When not busy at the hospital, he often helped other townsfolk, since most of the young boys and men had gone to join ranks with the Confederates to fight in the war.

Shaking linen to fold, Katherine asked, "Rosa, with all the fighting between the Gray and the Bluecoats going on around here, are you scared?"

"Yes, chile, we scared. But Thomas and I lived through bad times b'fo. Reckon we get through these times, too."

"Since you got your freedom, why do you stay here?"

"Chile, we got to do sumpin'. 'Sides, Mr. Duke good to us b'fo giving us our freedom. He says we can stay here as long as we wants to. He's payin' us to work and puttin' a roof over our heads. Reckon we doin' as good here as we could most anywheres."

"What if Lincoln's Union doesn't win the war, what will happen to you then?"

Rosa smiled and threw her hands up. "We trust de Lawd, chile. We done all right b'fo de war, and we'll do all right atta it's over."

She set another basket of linens up on the table to fold. "Does the war scare ya, Miss Katherine?"

Katherine paused from folding linens. "Yes, it does."

"Then, why ain't ya goin' home?"

"Mama wants me to, but if I stay here and work, it'll help pay my way for schooling. Mama wanted so bad to get me here. We just didn't know the war was going to break out here. If I leave now, I will lose my chance of gettin' a proper schoolin'. Mama says that with a good schoolin' I can better myself. Besides, there's one less mouth to feed at home with me gone."

"Your mama's a smart woman. She must be proud of ya."

Someone hollered from within the house. "Another wagon-load of wounded just rolled in! Everyone to the front porch!"

"You go hep'em, Miss Katherine. Me and Thomas will take care of this here washin'."

Katherine ran through the house to the front porch where she found Elizabeth and two other girls watching from the porch. Elizabeth, her roommate at the boarding school, had also stayed to help care for the wounded. They watched and listened with dread and anticipation to hear the conversation going on around the wagon.

A young man jumped from the wagon seat and walked to the back of the wagon where several townsmen had gathered to help. "We got us five on this wagon and three on the one that stopped up at the Tavern. Two of 'em died before getting here, so you got three here to take care of."

Another man stood at the wagon, shook his head and said, "Let's get 'em inside before they bleed to death. They won't last long lying on this wagon."

One at a time, the wounded soldiers were carried from the wagon, grunting and groaning with pain. As the last boy was unloaded and carried onto the porch, Katherine followed, holding the door open for them as they carried in an unconscious boy, his gray uniform ragged, torn, and filthy with powder burns and bloodstains.

Before entering the house, she heard, "Take these two and bury them. Save their belongings. Someone may come by asking for them later."

Katherine followed the two men carrying the young boy up the steps to the third floor where they turned left and made their way to the room on the right. They laid him on a table covered with clean linens, as Doc Foster, an older gentleman with a gray beard and wearing glasses low on his nose, walked in.

After examining the young boy for a moment, Doc Foster leaned back, looked over his glasses, and said, "He's got a chunk of metal in his rib cage stuck between two ribs and a chunk of metal in his right shoulder. I need to cut them out before infection sets in." He glanced at Katherine and asked, "Can you help me? Everyone else is busy tending to the other two boys that were brought in."

"I reckon so. Just tell me what to do," she answered, realizing there was no one else.

"Tell Rosa to boil some water and bring it up. Take these scissors and cut his clothes off him. Wash and clean where he's bleeding." He barked the orders out. "I'm going to get my bag so we can start."

Katherine rushed downstairs calling out, "Rosa, I need you to boil some water and bring it to the room at the top of the steps." She ran back upstairs, nervously anticipating what was about to happen.

The young boy looked as though he was only a year or so older than she. Her heart pounding with anxiety, adrenaline pushing her on, she first removed his boots. Picking up the scissors, she began to cut off what was left of his shirt and pants. What had once been a uniform was now only filthy, tattered rags. She was very careful not to hurt him as he lay semiconscious, moaning in pain.

Rosa entered with clean cloths and a pan of hot water. Doc Foster followed with his medical bag. The doctor repeated his instruction. "Take these cloths and wash his wounds as clean as you can."

Katherine began wiping dried blood from his body. Doc Foster cleaned several shiny instruments with a liquid from a brown bottle, and then laid them on a clean cloth.

"Katherine, everyone else is busy downstairs. I can't wait for them to do this. Are you sure you're up to helping? Even though he's almost passed out, he's going to feel the pain, and it won't be pretty. I will need you to help hold him down so I can cut that metal out of him."

She wrung her hands nervously, biting her bottom lip, but replied, "I'll try."

"Take that piece of leather and put it between his teeth for him to bite on. You go to the top of the table, hold his arms back, and whatever you do, don't let go."

At that moment, Thomas entered the room. Doc Foster gave him instructions also. "Thomas, you hold his legs down. You've done this before?"

"Yessir." He firmly gripped the young boy's legs to hold him down.

Taking a bottle of liquid from his medical bag, Doc Foster opened it and poured it into the wound on the boy's chest. The liquid started foaming and the boy began to grunt and struggle to get free. Taking a knife with a very shiny blade and a round wooden handle, Doc Foster lowered it to the wound.

He looked up over the rim of his glasses, "You got'em, Katherine?"

"Yes, yes," was all she could say as she closed her eyes and tightly held his arms to her side.

The pain woke the boy up, making him struggle hard to break free. Katherine opened her eyes and saw him sweating and biting on the leather piece in his mouth. He continued to scream and jerk as Katherine strained with all her might to hold him down. Just when she felt she could no longer hold him, he went limp. She glanced over at Doc, who was looking at a piece of metal he had taken out.

"The boy must have run head-on into cannon fire. He's lucky to be alive. The metal only cracked a couple of ribs. While he's out, let me get that shoulder fixed also and get him sewn up."

Finally, he stepped back, looked at Katherine and said, "You did fine. We just need to get us some anesthesia, though." He turned away in frustration, muttering to himself. "I guess eventually these boys will kill each other off, and then the war will end."

A young girl rushed into the room, yelling, "Come quick, Doc Foster, one of the Bluecoats downstairs is having convulsions!"

Before he left, the doctor said to Katherine, "Get some clean water and bathe him all over. I'll send a couple of men up to get him over to the bed. If he wakes up before I get back, give him a sip of water."

A few minutes later, with a pan of fresh water beside her, Katherine began to bathe the comatose boy that lay before her. She noticed his muscular body as she washed him and wondered what his name was, doing all she could to make sure he was clean but being ever so gentle and careful not to hurt him.

The boarding school/hospital stayed lively all day with the three new wounded soldiers needing so much attention. Katherine stayed by the injured boy's side, giving him sips of water as he faded in and out of consciousness.

Finally, late in the evening, Doc Foster came back to check on the boy. Katherine watched closely as he examined him and then stepped back, a worried look on his face.

"How is he?" Katherine asked.

"Not good." He shook his head. "He's taking a fever. Get some cold, wet rags and bring them up. I was afraid this might happen with him having two open wounds. His body just can't compensate for two bad injuries at the same time."

Running downstairs, she grabbed some cloths from Rosa's basket, and then ran back up.

"Keep a wet cloth on his head and neck and wipe his body down every few minutes with a cold, wet cloth," Doc Foster said. "I'll have Thomas bring fresh, cold water up ever so often. If we don't break the fever, we're going to lose him." Looking at her, he asked, "Are you up to it?"

"Yes, I'll stay with him," she said, already placing wet towels over his body. A little nervous, she was determined to help this young boy who lay in her care, even though she didn't know him.

Hour after hour passed as Katherine continued to care for the young boy, who remained unconscious. Wiping the sweat from his body, Katherine jumped every time his body twitched or he mumbled something. She felt that whether he lived or died depended on what she did for him.

Nighttime had fallen, and an oil lamp lit the room as Rosa walked in.

Speaking softly, she said, "Miss Katherine, I notice you didn't come down fo supper, so's I brung some food up fo ya."

A worried look on her face, Katherine replied, "I didn't want to leave him alone. He needs me here."

"I understans, chile. Here, you sit and eat. I'll keep the wet cloths on him."

Katherine sat down, exhausted. As she ate, she asked, "Rosa, do you find it strange to be caring for the Bluecoats and Confederates at the same time?"

"We's all God's chillun'. He don't see no gray or blue." She shook her head. "Maybe some day there won't be no diffunce no more."

"I hope you're right. This fighting has got to stop."

"Give it time, chile, and it'll work out. We just got to trust the Lawd." Rosa turned to Katherine. "I've got me some beef broth in the kitchen. Been savin' it to make gravy. I'll heat it up and you can let him sip on that. Maybe it'll help break his fever."

"I hope so," Katherine said as she turned back to tending to her patient.

Even though she was worn out, she continued to rotate cold cloths on him and gave him water or broth to sip as often as she could throughout the night. Finally, completely spent from her task, she fell asleep while sitting in a bedside chair, her head and arms on the foot of his bed.

Katherine looked away from Spencer and stood up. She walked from the gazebo out to the sidewalk and looked down towards the railroad tracks as if anticipating someone coming from that direction. Strands of her auburn hair shifted and floated as a gentle breeze stirred through the back lot where they stood.

Spencer heard a noise from behind, glanced around, and saw a waitress on the pool deck. Thinking that a beverage would be good, he asked, "Katherine, would you like a bottle of water or tea to drink?"

"Yes, I suppose it's tea time. I'll go and prepare some for us."

Lifting his hand, he said, "No, I'll have some brought down to us." He walked out from under the gazebo and waved at the waitress. "Is it possible to get two iced teas brought down?"

From the pool deck, the waitress said, "I'll be glad to bring them down to you. I'll be back in a moment."

Spencer turned his attention back to Katherine, who had walked into the yard. He watched her while wondering about her story. *Why is she talking about herself and a boy named Sam during the Civil War here in Abingdon? Is it from a book that she has read, acting out some fantasy of hers by sharing the story with me? Maybe if we talk longer I can figure out who she is and what her motive is for telling me this story.*

Spencer turned at the sound of someone behind him and found the waitress walking into the gazebo with a tray and two glasses.

"Here are your iced teas."

He checked his back pocket, and then remembered putting his wallet in the room safe earlier. He had a twenty dollar bill in his coat pocket, but decided he wouldn't make the waitress go for change. "Thank you, can I charge it to my room? I didn't bring my billfold out."

"Sure, just sign the receipt with your room number." She handed him the receipt.

While Spencer signed the receipt, the waitress said with a smile, "You must be thirsty. I would've been glad to bring you a refill. You didn't have to order two."

"Only one is for me. The other is for my guest, Katherine." He turned to point to Katherine but didn't see her anywhere. Calling her name, he looked around. "Katherine...Katherine!" But she was nowhere in sight. Turning back to the waitress who stood there quietly watching, he asked, "Did you happen to see the young lady that I was talking to?"

Looking quizzically, she answered, "No, sir."

"She was just here in front of me when I turned and saw you walk up," he said, pointing to the yard. "She couldn't have walked away that fast."

Shaking her head, the waitress said, "I'm sorry. I never saw anyone."

Spencer paused, and then took the two iced teas. "Thanks for bringing them down."

"Certainly, let me know if you need something else."

Spencer sat down, rested his elbows on his legs and tried to figure out why Katherine suddenly walked away again. *How did she get away so fast without the waitress noticing her? After all, her dress and appearance would surely have drawn attention. And I still don't know who she is or what she's up to. When she speaks, she only refers to things back in the nineteenth century. In fact, she said nothing to me indicating anything about herself in present time. She has got to be one heck of a good storyteller.*

A thought suddenly occurred to him that made him look around self-consciously, as if someone nearby could have heard his thoughts and think he was going crazy. *Maybe she's one of the ghosts from the past that supposedly haunted the Inn.*

Putting his face in his hands, he thought, *Oh gosh, now I'm trying to convince myself I'm talking to a ghost. I don't need to be dealing with this right now. My life is already screwed up enough. Now I'm fascinated with some young girl telling me a story that happened almost one hundred and fifty years ago.*

Throwing his hands up in frustration, he packed his laptop and headed back to his room, wondering why he seemed to be the only one who knew anything about Katherine and when in the world would he see her again.

CHAPTER 6

On The Creeper Trail

In his room awhile later, Spencer sat at the desk with his laptop, writing from notes he had taken from Katherine's earlier conversation. Not sure how the story would evolve or if he could even use it once he found out who Katherine was and what her intentions were, he wrote anyway.

Once he started writing, however, the story she had shared with him easily turned into an interesting narrative. He wrote tirelessly, losing track of time as the words flowed. Finally, he leaned back from the desk to take a breather and glanced at the clock on the fireplace mantel. It was four o'clock, and he needed a break from writing for the last three hours. He remembered the nearby Creeper Trail. A glance out the window confirmed rain was a possibility, but he decided to try the trail anyway and grabbed the light green raincoat he had brought.

Hurriedly making his way to the corner of the block, he passed a bike shop and decided to rent a bike, knowing that he could cover a lot more distance riding than walking. He stepped inside the shop, where an older man in gray coveralls was making adjustments on a bike.

"Too late to rent a bike?" Spencer asked, putting his hands on the counter.

Looking up at Spencer, the man shook his head. "No, not at all. How long will you need it?"

"Just a couple of hours. I want to see as much of the trail as I can before it gets dark."

"We're open until six. If you can get it back by then, I'll charge you only for a day."

"No problem. How much is it?"

"Ten dollars." The man wiped his hands on a rag and walked toward the counter.

Reaching to his back pocket, Spencer again remembered leaving his wallet in the room safe. Earlier he had put a twenty-dollar bill in his front pocket, which he pulled out and handed to the older gentleman.

Opening the cash register, the man replied, "My son cleaned out the register earlier to make a deposit. I can give you ten ones or this ten with the corner torn off and stained with red dye."

"The ten is fine; I'll pass it on anyway." He put the bill in his coat pocket.

"Take your pick from the front row. All of them are good riders."

Selecting a black bike trimmed in silver, Spencer pulled it off the rack and mounted it. "It's been awhile since I've ridden a bike. I'll see you by six," he hollered as he rode away.

"Enjoy your ride, son!" the older man yelled back as Spencer rode across the railroad tracks, making a left turn to enter the Creeper Trail.

As open meadows, towering trees, and a golf course development zipped by, Spencer began to relax. His thoughts turned to Miriam and how much fun they used to have hiking trails, horseback riding, and even biking on many of the excursions they had enjoyed together. The last several years together had become difficult as their careers and the kids seemed to demand more of their time. Spencer wished that somehow they could enjoy those times together again.

Finally, Spencer realized that all he was doing was pedaling the bike and not enjoying the scenery, since his mind was so busy thinking first about Miriam and then about Katherine. When a drizzle began to fall, he turned the bike around and started back toward Abingdon. The fog began to roll in, so he pedaled faster now, made easier by the downward slope. The fog thickened by the minute, his visibility ahead becoming more obscured.

Suddenly, he saw someone in front of him walking in the middle of the trail. Approaching the figure, he yelled, "Bike coming!"

He barely missed the person, who made no effort to get out of his way. He glanced back and saw a young boy with his arm in a sling, walking with a white, birch stick in his hand. Figuring it best to stop and check on the boy, he pulled his bike over and waited for him to catch up.

The young boy finally limped up to where Spencer stood beside his bike. No more than seventeen or eighteen-years-old, he wore faded gray jeans, a tan flannel shirt with the right sleeve rolled up on his arm, and worn, black boots laced above his ankles. What looked like a homemade sling held his left arm against his body, and around his neck and over his shoulder was an auburn-colored scarf.

Spencer asked, "Are you all right? I didn't mean to pass so close to you."

Startled, the young man replied, "Reckon so."

Spencer pointed. "What happened to your arm?"

"I fell off a wagon and broke it. Was gettin' ready to go fight in the war, but they said I was no good to them with a busted arm." He took his free hand and rubbed his arm that was in the sling.

Spencer thought that was odd, but questions could wait. The rain was coming down harder, and he was anxious to get back to the comfort of the Inn.

"Can I help you get home?" he asked. "It's beginning to rain pretty hard now."

The boy seemed oblivious to the rain. "My home is in Galax, but I'm going to Abingdon. Got me a girl waitin' for me. The footpath from Damascus was the safest route. Nobody travels it much at night."

Spencer persisted, growing wetter and more miserable by the moment. "I don't mind helping you get to Abingdon."

The young boy shook his head. "No, I just have a short ways to go."

Suddenly, another biker came coasting down the trail and hollered, "Bike coming!" The young boy didn't move, so Spencer grabbed him and pulled him to the side just as the biker rode by them, missing the boy by only inches. The biker stopped and turned around. "Is everything okay? I didn't realize he wasn't stepping out of the way."

Spencer, wondering why the boy didn't seem to react to anything, turned and asked, "Are you okay?"

He stared back as if nothing happened. "Yes, I'm fine."

Spencer walked over to the biker. "I almost hit him, too. I'm not sure, but I think maybe he must have a hearing problem since he didn't move out of the way for me either."

"Can I help you with him?" He nodded his head toward the boy.

"No, I think he's fine, but thank you for stopping."

The biker pulled his raincoat and hood tighter. "Certainly. We need to get back to Abingdon or we're going to get soaked by this rain."

"I'm right behind you as soon as I know this boy is on his way."

"Okay. Have a nice day." He raised his hand in a goodbye.

Raising his hand, he returned the wave. "Thanks, you too."

Once the biker rode away, the young boy said, "Best I be moving on. I know my girl will be looking for me. I sent word to her a couple days ago and told her I was coming home. She'll be expecting me."

"My name is Spencer. What's yours, son?"

"Samuel, Samuel Foley."

"Well, Samuel, if you've been thinking about serving our country, I'm proud of you. Here is ten dollars I have." He pulled the money from his coat and put it in Samuel's hand. "Would like to give you more, but that's all I have. Buy yourself a hot meal on me."

The boy stared at Spencer without saying a word.

"We need to get moving. It's raining harder now. Sure you can make it in okay? We're still a half mile or so from Abingdon."

"Yeah, I just got a short ways to go." He started walking again.

"Good luck to you, son." Spencer got on his bike and continued to Abingdon, thinking it odd that this young boy was out on the trail, walking alone in the rain. Then, he thought, *Look at me; I'm out here in the rain, too.*

Spencer made his way back to the bike shop in what had become a downpour. With the bike returned, he hurried back to the Inn to find Allen and a couple of other men talking on the front porch.

"So you got caught in the rain, did you, Mr. Aubreys?" Allen called out.

"Yes, I sure did. Went on a bike ride up the trail; I should've checked the weather first to see how near the rain was." He began to shake some of the water off his raincoat before entering the Inn.

"Would you like me to grab a towel or blanket for you?" Allen suggested.

Spencer replied. "No, I'm good. I don't mind the rain. It's the temperature dropping so fast that got to me. Two hours ago, I was almost sweating riding a bike, and now it's at least twenty degrees colder."

"Yes, it's going to stay like this through Friday; then we have our first blast of winter." Stepping closer, Allen said, "Are you sure I can't get something to help you dry off? You're shivering. You must be miserable."

"No, I'm going in right now." He kicked off his shoes and picked them up. "I'll try not to track water in for you to have to clean up."

"You're fine, Mr. Aubreys. If you go out next time, remember we have umbrellas here. Just ask for one."

"Certainly will, thanks."

A few minutes later, Spencer stood in the shower with the hot water heating his chilled body. Finally, warm and refreshed, he stepped out of the shower, dried off, and put on the house robe. Sitting in front of the gas logs, he mashed his squeeze ball and wondered whether the young boy had made it home safely. Suddenly, he realized he hadn't eaten anything since breakfast.

Once dressed, he went down to the Inn's dining room. At a small table by the window, he reviewed the menu as the pouring rain almost drowned out the chatter among guests sitting at the other tables. He remembered he didn't like to eat alone.

"Good evening, my name is Janet," a voice said, snapping him back to reality. A middle-aged lady stood smiling at him. "May I start you off with a glass of wine or cocktail before dinner?"

"Yes, I think so. I'll have a glass of chardonnay, Chalk Hill, since you have it. I can give you my dinner order also."

After ordering, Spencer's mind went back to his earlier encounter with Katherine. He hoped he was not scaring her away by asking too many questions. But the story she spoke about, that seemed to have happened in another time and place, captivated him. He hoped he could find her again.

Janet brought the wine and a basket of bread. "You seem to be a man in deep thought."

Spencer sighed and leaned back from the table. "Actually, I am."

"Anything I can help with?" she asked with a smile.

"Probably not, unless you know something about a young girl I met here. Her name is Katherine Broadwater."

"No, I've never heard that name."

"She's a young girl, dresses somewhat differently, and speaks with a very distinct southern accent. I've seen her twice here at the Inn. I'm trying to write a story around what she has been telling me, supposedly about her life that took place when this inn was used as a hospital during the Civil War. But she kind of just walks off without any warning before I can schedule further interviews with her."

45

"Does anyone else you've spoken with know anything about her?"

"No, it seems no one else has seen or heard of her. I'm beginning to think I'm talking to a ghost." He half smiled, watching her reaction.

Laughing and tilting her head back, she said, "I'm sure you'll eventually find out who she is, Mr. Aubreys. Hopefully, she's not playing a game with you and leading you to believe she's someone she's not. There's a college up the road from here. Maybe she's from there and just fulfilling some sorority initiation. We hear of those things around here once in awhile. You know how kids are."

"I hadn't thought about that."

"She could even be a student who's doing a term paper on some event of history here in Abingdon and has chosen the Inn as her project. Maybe even a drama student writing a script for theater or a story for her creative writing class."

That perked him up. "I hadn't thought about any of that."

"Let me go get your entrée. Enjoy your dinner."

"Thanks for your help, Janet," he added as she walked away.

While eating, Spencer thought about what Janet had said concerning Katherine being a student and the possibilities for the story she had shared with him. It all seemed possible, then again, it didn't. Katherine always spoke so emotionally and sincerely, as if she were a girl from another time and place. All of that mystified him. *I must find her and see what she's up to*, Spencer concluded as he continued eating.

After dinner, sitting in his room in front of the gas logs, Spencer read from his laptop what he'd written earlier from Katherine's conversation up to the point when she walked away. Knowing that without her he wouldn't be able to continue the manuscript, he began thinking how to go about finding her.

He searched the telephone book for the name Broadwater, hoping to find a number that would lead him to her. But the name was not listed, and knowing that no one around the Inn seemed to know her, he remembered his earlier conversation with Bernice about helping. Finding her card on the table, he gave her a call.

After several rings, she answered. "Good evening, Bernice here."

"Hello, Bernice. This is Spencer."

"Hi, Spencer. Have you found anything you want to write about yet?"

"Actually, I have. Not sure how it's going to end, but I think I'm onto something good." He eased back in the chair in front of the gas logs. "I remember you telling me that this inn was a girl's boarding school in the nineteenth century but was used as a hospital during the Civil War."

"Yes, that's correct."

"I'm trying to get in contact with a young lady I met and talked to earlier. She's telling me a story about a girl and boy that took place here at the Inn when it was used as a hospital. I know it sounds strange, but she almost has me convinced the story is real. I need to find her to get the rest of her story."

"That's interesting. Who is she?"

"Her name is Katherine Broadwater. I've already spoken to her twice. She left before I could get information on how to contact her, though. I thought maybe you could help me locate her."

"Have you checked the telephone directory or asked around to see if anyone knows her?"

Picking up his squeeze ball and mashing it, he said, "Yes, I have. No one knows her, and there's no Broadwater listed in the directory."

"What does she look like?"

Rubbing his forehead, he remembered, "A young girl, no more than fifteen or sixteen years old. She has long, auburn colored hair, and both times that I met her she was dressed in what looked like an old-fashioned dress and spoke with a very southern accent."

"Then she is young?"

"Yes, she is, but seems very mature for her age."

"What's the story about?"

Spencer lifted his feet to the footstool and relaxed even more into the chair.

"The story is about a girl and a boy named Sam, who was a Confederate soldier, and their life during the Civil War. She claims to be the girl in this story and sounds so convincing." He paused to let that sink in. "I'm not sure if I'll be able to use her story, but she's one interesting person, and I want to at least try."

"That's interesting. I'll check records of both Abingdon and the surrounding counties to see if I can find any Broadwater listed."

"Thanks for your effort, Bernice. While you're at it, could you maybe check with the Historical Society here and see if they have any records with names of the girls who attended this boarding school during the Civil War? Maybe there was a girl with that name who attended the school, and she has concocted a story from something she knows or has read about her. You have my number if you learn anything."

"That's a good idea, Spencer. I will check with them. They should have records."

"Thanks for your effort. Good night."

As Bernice hung up the telephone, she began to think, *Maybe I need to call Elaine and tell her what Spencer has asked me to do. I'm just not comfortable with him asking me to help find a fifteen- or sixteen-year-old girl.* She dialed Elaine's number.

Elaine answered after three rings. "Hello, Bernice, glad you called. I was wondering how the meetings between you and Spencer have been going."

"We only met once, on Tuesday evening, when he got here."

"What do you think about him?"

"He seemed to be tuned into what I shared with him. He mostly took notes and didn't ask a lot of questions."

"Then he must have gotten the information he needed."

Sitting down and resting her elbow on a table, Bernice said, "The reason I'm calling is that he just called me with a strange request." She paused, not sure how to tell Elaine.

"What was it?"

"He asked me to help find a young lady he met and spoke with a couple of times at the Inn."

"What for?" Elaine asked.

"Something about that she had shared parts of her life's story with him. She claimed to be a girl named Katherine Broadwater in a story that's about her and a boy named Sam during the Civil War here in Abingdon. He wanted to interview her further so he could continue writing the story. I'm sure his intentions are good, but I wasn't sure if finding her for him was the right thing to do, since she is so young."

"I've known Spencer for years. I know his intentions are what he said they were. Why don't you see if you can locate this young lady, but you call her and let her contact Spencer if she so desires."

"That's a good idea," Bernice agreed. "I'll try to find her and get back to you."

"Very well. Call me if you think I need to know anything else about what's going on."

"Thanks for your help. I look forward to seeing you this weekend."

CHAPTER 7
Better Acquainted

Thursday morning was again cloudy and foggy. Spencer stretched for a few minutes before rolling out of bed. As he stood in front of the gas logs to warm up, his thoughts again turned to Miriam and their broken marriage. *Did she go out on a date with someone else and, if so, would that finalize their separation? What could he possibly say that would win her back?*

After a shower, he dressed and went downstairs to the dining room for breakfast.

Yesterday's breakfast waitress greeted him. "Good morning, Mr. Aubreys, would you like coffee and juice again?"

"Yes, in fact, I will have the same as yesterday."

"Good, I'll get it started." She turned up his cup and poured the steaming coffee.

"You must have a good memory."

"No, not at all," she shook her head. "We just don't have many guests right now, so it's easy to remember. I'll have breakfast right out."

Spencer realized he hadn't turned on his phone to check messages at all for Wednesday, so he turned it on. A message rang in, which was a call from Miriam.

"Hello, Spencer, it's Miriam. I just wanted you to know that I wasn't trying to pry into your business when we talked yesterday. Hope I didn't come across that way." A pause, then, "Also, I wanted to let you know I didn't take the invitation for the date. Hope you enjoy your time at the Inn. Call me when you get home, and tell me about it when you have time. Bye."

The waitress placed a plate of food in front of him, "Here's your breakfast, Mr. Aubreys. Let me know if you need anything."

"Certainly will and thank you," he answered.

Relieved and feeling better since he had gotten the phone message from Miriam, Spencer began to think. *So she didn't go out with that guy. Maybe she's beginning to think that our marriage is worth saving.*

Spencer finished breakfast and on his way from the dining room he stopped at the gift shop.

"Looking for a gift for someone?" the clerk asked after watching him browse for a while.

"Just a souvenir, I guess. What would you suggest?"

"The Christmas ornaments or a print of the Inn are the two most popular."

Spencer thought, *I wouldn't want to get the print unless Miriam was here sharing the trip with me.* "Let's go for the ornament." He brought one to the register. "Do you have a box for it?"

"Sure. Would you like for me to wrap it?"

Shaking his head, he said, "No, but a small gift bag would be good."

As she wrapped it in tissue, she asked, "A gift for a special friend?"

Spencer paused and then replied, "Yes, it could be, or I hope so."

Back in his room, Spencer looked out the window and observed the heavy traffic and people walking on the street below. No one wore a coat, so he decided that another day outside on the patio or gazebo would be a good place to do some writing since it apparently had warmed up. He reached to get his laptop and notes and noticed the flower that Katherine picked earlier had begun to wilt, so he added more water to the glass and placed it back on the table.

He slipped into a sweat shirt and, with laptop in hand, went outside to the gazebo. Thoughts of Katherine brought him to the spot where he had seen her before. Temporarily forgetting his

51

problems with Mariam, his thoughts went back to how to solve the mystery of who Katherine was and what her motive was for the story she had shared with him.

After several minutes, he was surprised to see Katherine standing, watching him from the gazebo, as if purposely waiting for him.

Spencer walked over quietly and leaned against one of the gazebo columns. Katherine stood straight, not saying a word, but watched him closely.

Finally, he spoke. "Good morning, Katherine, I'm glad you came by today. I was kind of surprised when you left so suddenly yesterday." He watched, intensely anticipating her answer.

She stared at him, without blinking an eye, as she spoke. "Yes, I had chores to do and needed to start getting things ready for when Sam returns. So much for one to do, you know."

"Katherine, you aren't from around here, are you?" He dived right in. "You act different, dress different, and even speak with a different accent. Tell me the truth. Who are you and what are you up to?"

Katherine glanced away, paused and looked back at him, a confused look on her face. "My name is Katherine. I'm not up to anything." She lifted her hands, clasped them together, and took a couple of steps back. "I'm waiting for Sam to come home."

Frustrated, Spencer stepped closer and spoke firmly. "Katherine, what are you up to? This tale you speak of about you and some boy named Sam that happened during the War Between the States here in Abingdon makes no sense. Is this from some book you have read or a movie you have seen that you are trying to act the part? Why do you think I am gullible enough to believe this fantasy or concoction that you are telling me? What is your purpose for making this up?"

The tone in his voice, bordering on anger, surprised even him.

She stared down and shook her head. "I don't understand. I'm just waiting for Sam. He should be here soon. By Friday is what his note said." She glanced up, tears in her eyes.

Spencer backed away, realizing that he was upsetting her. He held up his hands. "I didn't mean to upset you." Knowing that he had spoken to her too aggressively, he pondered what he should say or do. Finally, he said, "Here, take my handkerchief."

Katherine wiped the tears from her face, clutched the handkerchief to her bosom and stared down, not saying a word.

Feeling guilty, Spencer shuffled around momentarily, trying to find the right words to apologize.

"Look, I'm sorry. There's no excuse for me to have talked to you like I did." He held out his hand. "Here, come in and sit down for a moment."

Opposite each other on the benches, Spencer said, "Katherine, I shouldn't have spoken to you as I did. I'm just so stressed out, dealing with a lot of other problems in my life that's gone wrong. Now you show up telling me this story and then do a disappearing act on me. I'm totally confused. I can't eat, sleep or breathe without thinking about you, or some problem in my life."

Katherine nodded in agreement as she continued to wipe tears and compose herself.

Spencer sat silently for a moment, staring down and thinking. *Here I sit with a girl no one else knows anything about. How do I get her to open up about herself and tell me who she is? Do I stay here and go along with her act or do I leave? If I stay, will I get a story from her?*

After a few minutes, he decided he had nothing else to write about, so he quietly said, "Do you feel better now?"

Relaxing, she dropped her hands to her lap. "Yes, I think so."

"Would you like to tell me about Sam? Is he going to be okay? I would like to know more about him if you're up to talking about him."

She glanced downhill from the gazebo before quietly beginning. "I hope Sam makes it home soon. I have good news to tell him. I need him here with me."

"Yes, tell me about Sam." Spencer reached for his laptop.

Startled, Katherine sprang up to a sitting position when she heard a loud knock on the door. Realizing that she had fallen asleep earlier, she felt embarrassed when Doc Foster entered the room.

"Didn't mean to scare you," he said, setting his bag down. "I just wanted to see if the boy made it through the night."

Katherine glanced over at the patient and was surprised to find him staring at her with a half grin on his face. She awkwardly replied to the doctor, "Yes, I think he might be coming around. I fed him water and some of Rosa's broth all night. I fell asleep a short while ago, I guess."

"Rosa's broth will either kill you or cure you. Looks as if it did the latter for you, son," Doc Foster said.

"Yeah, I reckon so," the boy replied weakly.

Doc Foster turned to Katherine. "I'm going to check him out and change the dressings on his wounds. Why don't you take a break? Grab a bite to eat or whatever you need to do while I examine him."

"Yes, I think I will." Katherine glanced back at the wooden poster bed and caught the boy staring at her.

On her way downstairs, she met Elizabeth coming down the hallway.

"Good morning, Katherine. I didn't see you come down to bed last night."

"I stayed up all night taking care of one of the boys brought in yesterday. Doc Foster had to cut some metal out of him. He took a fever, so I stayed up and gave him water and broth to sip to break his fever." She brushed some straggling strands of hair from her face.

Elizabeth was from a well-to-do family that lived nearby. A year or so older than Katherine, she was tall with long, black hair, dark eyes, and a slim figure. She was a beautiful girl who loved the attention she received from all the young men she encountered.

"Who is he?" Elizabeth asked, her arms crossed, leaning against the staircase arm rail.

"I'm not sure. I haven't spoken with him yet. He was awake when I came down, but Doc Foster was tending to him." Katherine ran her fingers through her hair to evenly shift it over her shoulders. "He was one of the Confederates brought in on the wagon yesterday."

"I sat and tended to a Union soldier for a while last night," interjected Elizabeth. "Said he was from Pittsburgh, Pennsylvania, wherever that is. He's an officer with the Union Army and likes music. I'm going to play my violin for him later." She raised her arms to the air as though she were already playing.

Turning towards the kitchen, Katherine said, "That's good, but I need to see if Rosa needs my help in the kitchen."

In the kitchen, Rosa was singing while slicing peeled apples and tossing them into a bucket.

Katherine grabbed an apron from the wall hook. "Good morning, Rosa. What can I do to help?"

Glancing at Katherine, she stopped singing. "Morning, chile, looks like ya been up most of the night."

After pouring water from a bucket to a basin, Katherine began washing her hands. "Yes, I was awake until about daybreak, then I dozed off."

"How's that boy doin'?"

Katherine dried her hands on her apron. "Doc's looking at him now. He was awake when I came down. His fever must've broken, I reckon."

Rosa pointed to two pots of food on the stove top. "Want to take him sumpin' to eat?"

"Yes, I suppose I can do that." Picking up a tin plate, she walked to the stove, trying to figure out where to start.

Rosa's back was to Katherine as she sliced apples. "There's grits in the pot and warm biscuits in the oven. Cut'em off a piece of side meat, and there's fresh milk in the cold box."

Katherine began getting the food together.

"'Lizabeth seems excited 'bout the Bluecoat she's tending to," Rosa said.

Katherine sighed. "Yes, she stopped me in the hallway and told me about him."

"Hope nothin' comes out of it. Her daddy won't like her takin' to a Bluecoat." Rosa shook her head at that thought.

"Maybe she's just fascinated because he showed her some attention." Placing her hands on her hips, she turned toward Rosa. "You know how Elizabeth is, she loves a chase. Hopefully he'll be gone soon."

Rosa shooed her with her hand. "You run along and take food to da boy. When ya comes back down, I'll be afixin' breakfast. Ya need to eat and get some rest, too."

Katherine picked up the tray of food. "Rosa, you sound like my mama."

"Just tryin' to look after ya, chile," she said with a chuckle.

Upstairs again, Katherine found Doc Foster bandaging the young boy's chest and shoulder as he sat up in bed. She stopped and stared, now noticing his thick, brown, wavy hair falling down his neck and his strong, muscular face. When he glanced up at her, his dark-brown eyes held her in a trance.

"Son, you are a lucky man," Doc told him. "You lost a lot of blood, and if that metal in your rib cage had gone in another quarter inch, it would've punctured your lung. There would've been no saving you then."

The boy ignored Doc and shifted his eyes toward Katherine, and asked, "When can I leave?"

Doc spoke more firmly, staring at the young soldier over the rim of his glasses. "It's going to take at least two weeks for those ribs to start mending and possibly several weeks before you're back to normal. You need to stay still and rest for at least the next several days. You lost a lot of blood."

Katherine stood fixated as the boy continued to stare at her and argue with Doc Foster. "But I got to get back to the militia. They need me," he said.

"You should've thought about that before running head on into cannon fire," Doc said in an even firmer voice.

Doc glanced at Katherine. "I see you brought him something to eat. I'm not getting through to him, anyway. I'm going to check on the others." He turned before walking out the door. "Make sure he stays in bed."

Katherine stood with the tray of food and stared at the boy. He stared back with a half grin on his face. She searched for words to say.

Finally, she set the tray down on a stand and suggested, "Maybe if I put another pillow behind your head, it'll be easier to eat."

"Maybe so," he agreed.

Taking a pillow, she carefully raised him up as he moaned and winced with pain. She stopped because he looked so uncomfortable.

"I'm sorry," she said.

"I can't help it. I'm sore and it hurts," he said, trying to lean forward again.

After another attempt, she succeeded in getting two pillows behind him and placed the tray of food on the bed beside him.

"Can you reach it?" she asked.

He reached for the food and again winced in pain, then relaxed back into bed. "I'm so sore it hurts to even breathe."

"I'll feed you." Katherine sat in the chair by his side and began to spoon grits to him.

While eating, he stared at Katherine and finally spoke. "How long were you here last night?"

"I've stayed with you since they pulled you off the wagon yesterday."

"Don't remember much of anything. Last I saw was a flash of light, and then woke to find you sleeping and all slumped over on my bed."

"Must have been the cannon fire you walked into," she said with a frown.

"We shoulda seen it comin'. Heard 'em on the ridge, 'cross the hollow. Then it got real quiet. We thought they must've left. Couldn't see because of the fog. They were waitin' for us, and when they heard us comin' up the hill, they opened fire with cannon. They fight like cowards."

She was silent for a minute as she spooned him more grits. "Why do y'all do all this fighting and killing? Nobody wins, and a lot of men and boys get killed."

"Ain't got no choice. They come down here trying to take what's ours. If we work for it, then we should have the right to keep it."

Katherine cut a piece of side meat and forked it to him. "I'll be glad when the war's over. Everybody's scared. We don't know what's coming."

He took the side meat and pointed toward the cup on the tray. "Can I have a drink of that milk?"

Katherine gave him the milk. He gulped down half a cup before handing it back.

Cutting another piece of side meat with the knife and wanting to change the subject, she asked, "What's your name?"

Grinning, he said, "You can call me Sam. What's yours?" He began chewing on the meat.

"Katherine...Katherine Broadwater." She focused on him with narrowed eyes. "How long did you lie awake and watch me this morning?"

"Not long. I wasn't sure where I was. Thought maybe the Bluecoats had captured me. Tried to get up, but I was hurtin' too bad. Just where might I be?"

"You're in Abingdon. This was a boarding school for girls. But so many boys and men were getting hurt, so they turned it into a hospital. Some of us girls are staying here to help."

Sam swallowed hard and asked, "Where's your home?"

"Mama and Papa live on a ridge near here called Copper Creek. About a day's ride west of here," she answered, pointing with her finger.

Sam shifted over to the left side of the bed to get closer. "Why didn't you go home when the war started?"

"Mama and Papa are having hard times now. They have six other young'uns to feed. Papa lost his job in the salt mines when the Union closed them down. If I go home, it would be just another mouth to feed. Besides, I'm working my way through school here so I can get me a good education."

Sam shrugged his shoulders. "What do you need schoolin' for?"

"Mama said if I get me a proper schooling, then I can better myself." She raised her chin up proudly.

Sam turned his head and thought for a second, then looked back and said, "A woman don't need schoolin' to do farm chores, raise kids, and keep house, do ya?"

Katherine laid the fork on the tray and snapped at him. "Maybe I'm aiming to do something with my life besides chores, housework, and raise kids."

"Didn't mean to get you all riled up," Sam said, a confused look on his face.

"One of these days we women are going to make a difference. You'll see. We are just as smart as you men." She slapped her leg with a hand.

He retorted, "You can't work like us men do. Harness the mule to plow the ground, cut the timber, or skin a steer for food."

Katherine stood up, placed her hands on her hips and answered sharply. "Well, at least you don't see us women running head-on into cannon fire. And who has to take care of you once you're all shot up?" She picked up the food tray and walked toward the door.

"Where're you goin' with the rest of that food?" He pointed at the tray. "I'm still chewin' on that side meat."

Turning around, Katherine looked at him angrily and said, "I'm going to milk the cows, wash the clothes, and make a baby. After all, that's what I'm supposed to do, ain't it?" She stomped out the room.

Back in the kitchen, Katherine dumped the food scraps into the slop bucket, and then started washing plates without saying a word. Grabbing pots and pans and scrubbing them furiously, she quietly fumed at the nerve of the boy.

Rosa watched for a few minutes, and then softly said, "Got ya a plate of food on the table. Better eat b'fo it gets cold."

Since Rosa had gone out of her way to prepare a good breakfast, Katherine sat down and began eating.

Before she finished, Rosa sat down, too. She asked, "Sumpin' get you riled up?"

Rolling her eyes, Katherine replied, "Men! Always saying the wrong things. They don't appreciate us women. They think we're helpless."

"No, chile, men likes us. They just slow 'bout showin' us. Sooner or later, they comes 'round. You and that boy upstairs ain't havin' words, is ya?"

"He just said a woman's place is to do farm chores, house cleaning, and raise kids."

Rosa turned up her head and laughed. "Lawdy, chile, ya don't even know the boy and y'all already fightin'. That's not a good sign at all. He's just messin' wit ya 'cause he likes ya. Mercy, I sees I need to keep you two apart."

Katherine took her plate to the sink. She turned back to Rosa. "Do I need to take food to any of the other men?" she asked.

"No, I bleves we got 'em all fed." She pointed to the corner. "Why don'tcha take the slop bucket out to Thomas? He can feed them hogs. Then, go get yoself some rest b'fo we starts feedin' agin."

Katherine took the slop bucket out to Thomas. On the way back to her room, she stopped to pick fresh flowers from a bush. Always fascinated by the fragrance and beauty of flowers, she rubbed the petals between her fingers and lifted the blossoms to her nose. Smiling, she thought. *These will look nice and smell good in my room.*

A few minutes later, in her room, she placed the flowers in a small vase of water. After she got undressed, she found herself thinking about Sam.

She went to her trunk, unlocked it, and lifted out her diary. It had been a gift from her mother more than a year ago when she left home to come to the boarding school. Opening it once again, she read the words her mother wrote to her.

Katherine, it tears my heart to see you leave home. But you are almost fourteen, and I know that if you don't get a proper schooling, you'll end up on the side of a mountain with a house full of babies like me. I wouldn't trade it for anything, but I want all my children to have a chance for a better life. You got to have schooling to make it happen. I know that someday soon you will be a woman. It's nothing you can plan for. It just happens. Write your moments, both of joy and pain into this here diary. Someday you will look back and cherish them. Also, your children and their children will someday read them and be able to reach back in time and see what a wonderful and beautiful woman you are.

Love,

Mama

Katherine picked up her quill, dipped it into the ink bottle, and wrote her moments for the day.

Five Confederate soldiers were brought to the school yesterday. Two died before getting here. I helped tend to a boy named Sam. I helped Doc Foster cut two pieces of metal from cannon fire out of him. I almost fainted with all the bleeding and screaming he was doing. I sat up all night with him trying to help him break a fever. Fell asleep and woke up with him staring at me.

Rosa is slicing apples to dry so we can eat fried apple pies this winter. Elizabeth has taken to a Yankee soldier. I hope her pa doesn't find out.

Sam is, well, kind of high strung, looks as strong as an ox and probably wild as a buck. Kind of says what's on his mind, whether I like it or not. He looks to be sixteen or seventeen years old, not bad looking. In fact, he's kinda cute.

Got to go to sleep. It's been a long day.

CHAPTER 8
A Truce

Spencer stopped writing and asked, "So you have a diary that has this story in it?"

"Yes, Mama gave it to me when I left home to come here to the boarding school."

Hoping he could now get Katherine to finally expose who she was and what her intentions were, Spencer decided to question her. Putting his laptop down and leaning forward, he asked pointedly, "Is this the boarding school you are talking about?" He gestured towards the Inn.

She nodded, "Yes, Elizabeth and I share a room here."

Sitting upright, thumping the bench he sat on, he said, "Katherine, your story is wonderful. But is it something you've read from someone's diary from long ago?"

She shook her head, "Other girls here have diaries, I suppose. But no one would dare read them or have a reason to."

Spencer decided to ask a few history questions to see how she responded. "Do you know what today's date is?"

"Yes, it's November 11, 1863. Sam will be home come Friday."

Spencer shook his head at her seeming sincerity, and then picked up his laptop so he wouldn't miss a thing she said.

"What year were you born?"

"I was born in 1849. I'm the oldest girl in my family."

Spencer glanced up and asked, "What are the names of your mother and father?"

"My papa's name is Zack, named after Papa Zackary. My mama's name is Clara." She smiled.

Spencer raised his finger to his chin thinking. *She even has her personal life down to wanting me to believe she is from the nineteenth century. I have to give her credit. She doesn't miss anything.*

Then he asked, "Who is our president now, and what number is he in our line-up of presidents?"

Without hesitation, Katherine said. "It's Jefferson Davis. He's been our president since 1861 and is our first president."

"Where's the capital where our president lives?"

"Richmond, Virginia, now. But it was first in Montgomery, Alabama."

Spencer sat back and stared at Katherine through narrowed eyes and thought, arguing back and forth with himself.

It's as if she really is living in the past. It's obvious something's not normal about her. Her accent is different, she's worn the same dress all three times I've seen her, and now this story she's telling that was supposed to have happened in the 1860s. I have yet to hear her say anything about present-day Abingdon. If I believed in ghosts, I would swear that she is one. But aren't all the stories about the ghosts living here at the Inn just tales to get tourists' attention?

I need to make sure someone else sees Katherine with me today. I'll just watch her closely so she won't have a chance to walk off again. I have to admit she's telling one convincing story, though. I only hope I can use it and not find out that it's someone else's story that she has gotten her hands on from somewhere.

He was getting nowhere with his thoughts, so he decided to resume writing where she'd left off.

"Katherine, tell me more about Sam. Is he going to recover from his wounds?"

Smiling, Katherine sighed and perked up when she resumed talking about Sam.

Thunder rumbled from a distance and dark skies released huge raindrops on Abingdon. Katherine and Elizabeth ran from the clothesline, their arms full of bed linens that had been hanging since early morning. Making it to the back porch before the rain drenched them, they began to fold and stack the linens.

Elizabeth asked, "Have you been back to see Sam today? Everyone said he's asking about you."

Katherine picked up a linen sheet and shook it. She replied, "No, I haven't. We kinda had words about the war and all yesterday. Figured it best if I stayed away."

"You know, he's kinda cute, especially when he looks at you with those dark brown eyes." She eyed Katherine closely.

"Most young boys are cute," Katherine quickly snapped back, avoiding Elizabeth's eyes.

Elizabeth changed the subject. "The Union officer I'm tending said they're going to win the war. It's just a matter of time."

"How does he know that?" Katherine asked.

"Because they're sending more infantry down every day. They're stopping all rail service to keep supplies from coming up through the south. They have already closed the salt mines, so the south can't get salt for their fresh meat."

"Why are they doing that? They're hurting a lot of folks who have nothing to do with the war. Papa lost his job in the salt mine, and he has done nothing against them," she scowled.

Rosa opened the door and called, "Can one of you come and help me get de food to da rooms?"

Katherine replied, "Go help, Elizabeth. I'll stay here and finish folding the linens and bring them in so they can finish drying."

While she worked, a couple of men in gray uniforms rode up on horseback from the back lot and tied their horses. As they approached the porch, she realized she had never seen them before.

They walked up to the porch and removed their hats. "Morning, ma'am."

Katherine stepped toward them and said, "You better come up on the porch or you're going to get wet."

"Thank you, ma'am, but reckon we best stay down here and out of sight. Don't want to upset them Bluecoats you have there in the hospital. The judge and sheriff are supposed to meet us back here shortly."

Judge Grey, the judge who presided over the town's court and Sheriff Bradley, the town's sheriff, walked out from around the house and down to greet them. They walked away to a large poplar tree to get out of the rain and out of sight, but Katherine overheard their conversation.

"Evening, fellas, have any trouble on the way in?" Judge Grey asked.

"No, we came in by way of the footpath from Damascus. It's too narrow for the Yanks to travel. I'm not sure they even know about it," one of the men replied.

Sheriff Bradley asked, "How's it looking for you out there?"

"The Union has a steady flow of militias and supplies coming down from the north. They're crossing the mountain at Charlottesville and following the western slope all the way down. They're sabotaging the rail tracks as they move south."

The other stranger added, "They're gonna make sure no supplies can get to the Confederates from the south. If they think someone is harboring, or has something the Confederates could use, they either take it or burn it. It doesn't matter what it is or whose it is."

"What has me worried," Sheriff Bradley added, "is that the fighting is getting closer to Abingdon every day. If they knew we had our own militia, they would doubtless come in and burn us down."

"It's just a matter of time," the stranger replied. "They know they have the freedom to take what they want and to do what they want. They don't need a reason. When they get ready to raid you, you won't have a chance."

"It's getting hard to protect the militia. I'm afraid they're gonna raid the hospital and arrest the Confederates we're caring for," Sheriff Bradley added.

"Just make sure once they're able to travel, get them out through the underground tunnels. We'll get 'em back to Damascus by way of the footpath."

"Also, make sure no one wears any of the gray uniforms while here. Union soldiers would probably shoot 'em on sight."

Judge Grey added with concern, "It's dangerous times now. It wouldn't take much for us to have a full war goin' on here. Everyone's on edge, so keep everything quiet about what we're doing trying to aid you."

"Let us know when more men are ready to travel, we'll come for them. Okay, everyone knows what to do. Remember, no discussing plans with anyone. Let's split up."

The two strangers walked back to their horses. Judge Grey and Sheriff Bradley walked around to the side of the house and out of sight.

Katherine thought about what was said, not realizing things had gotten so bad. *Maybe Sam was right. He has no choice but to fight. Maybe I was too hard on him.* She finished folding the linens and carried them into the house, determined to go back to see him that night.

Finally, after finishing her chores and working into the night, Katherine decided to go visit Sam, and picked up the vase of fresh flowers she had gathered earlier.

Walking the three flights of stairs to his room, she stopped at the door to see if he was awake. An oil lamp burned, and he lay with his good arm under his head, staring up at the ceiling. She stood at the door and knocked to get his attention.

A smile lit up his face when he saw her. "Katherine, come in. I was hoping to see you again."

She held up the vase of fresh cut flowers as she walked toward him. "I want to propose a truce. I won't pick on you for fighting in the war, if you won't pick on me for being a woman." She set the vase of flowers on a dresser.

Sam laughed. "Sounds fair enough to me."

She smiled. "How are you feeling?"

"Sore as hell. Doc Foster wants me to start walking around some. Just can't do no liftin' for a couple of weeks."

"Anything I can do for you before I leave?"

"Yep." With a big smile, he asked, "How about takin' a seat and settin' for a spell?"

"I can manage a few minutes, but I need to turn in early so I can help Rosa with the cooking in the morning." She stifled a yawn.

"They told me you helped Doc Foster cut the lead out of me. I'm grateful."

"I almost fainted twice. Didn't let him know it though."

"You know, I been thinkin' 'bout you ever since I woke up and saw you. Was lying here hurtin' real bad, but didn't want to wake you, 'cause I thought you might leave."

"I would've come back if invited," Katherine answered with a smile. Clasping her hands in her lap, she said, "Tell me about yourself and your family."

"Pa and Joe, my older brother, and me got us a spread in Galax, 'bout four days' ride from here. We raise steers and cut timber for the railroad. When the war started, the Union stopped the railroad from buying our timber. They said the railroad would be siding with the south in the war if they done business with southerners. Every time those Yankees came through, they'd kill off some of our steers for food. Said they have the right to seize what they want. That's the reason I'm fightin' them. It's not fair."

"I can understand. How about your mama? What's she like?"

"I was young when she passed on. I can't remember a lot about her. Pa and Joe raised me and did the best they could." He continued with a smile, "Pa named Joe and me after men in the Bible. I was named after Samuel and Joe was named after Joseph. Pa calls us Joe and Sam. Pa made us go to church all the time and made us learn how to read and write. Said we'll thank him for it someday."

"He must be a really good man," Katherine replied.

"Yeah, he didn't want me goin' off and fightin'. Hope the war ends soon so I can go home and be with my family again." Sam paused as if remembering, then turned to Katherine. "Tell me about your family."

She smoothed her dress in her lap before beginning. "We have a big family. I have six brothers and sisters. I'm the oldest girl. Papa raises steers also and used to work in the salt mines until the Union closed them down. Mama got me in the boarding school a year before the war started. Been here nearly two years now."

"Looks like the war is affectin' all of us," Sam said, stifling a yawn.

"Yes, it is." Standing and stretching her arms, she yawned again. "Well, it's been nice talking to you, Sam. I need to go down and turn in. Be morning before you know it."

"Doc wants me to start walking around tomorrow." Reaching over and touching her arm, he asked softly, "How 'bout walkin' with me and showin' me the town?"

"I can do that after I finish my work."

"Then I'll see you in the morning?" Sam smiled.

"Yes, you probably will." She smiled one more time and nodded her head.

Violin music could be heard from somewhere. Sam glanced around. "Where is that music comin' from?"

Katherine waved her hand toward the door. "That's Elizabeth. She's playing for one of the Bluecoats downstairs."

"It sounds pretty. Shame to waste it on a Bluecoat."

"Yes, she's gifted. Hopefully, he's gonna be gone soon."

Sam glanced at the flowers. "Thanks for the flowers. They help brighten this room."

Katherine turned and looked at them as she stepped to the door. "I'm glad you like them."

"Good night, Katherine. Would you mind turning down the lamp?"

She reached over to the dresser and turned the wick down until the light went out. Turning to leave the room, she said, "Good night, Sam."

Quietly making her way downstairs and down the hallway, she passed the room where Elizabeth had been playing the violin. The door was closed, but she heard a giggle from inside. Pausing for a moment, she frowned, and then moved on.

Once inside her room, she went to her trunk and got her diary to write that day's entry.

I visited with Sam this evening. He now has color back in his cheeks. His long, wavy, brown hair and dark-brown eyes do kind of catch your attention. Maybe Elizabeth is right—when he looks at me, I melt.

I am afraid for Elizabeth taking to a Bluecoat with all the fighting and anger going on against them. Hope her pa doesn't find out about her taking a liking to him.

Got to get some rest. It's my turn to help Rosa with the cooking in the morning.

CHAPTER 9
The Walk

"Swing low, sweet chariot, Comin' fo to carry me home, Swing low," Rosa sang, as Katherine walked into the kitchen. With her hair tied back, she was dressed in a full-length, light-green dress with white lace around her neckline. She picked up an apron, slipped it over her head and tied it in the back.

Rosa stopped singing. "Morning, chile. Ya look all spruced up and prettier than a heifer calf this morning."

"Morning, Rosa. I just wanted to look nice today. A girl doesn't have much of a chance to dress up anymore with the war going on, especially with all the work we have to do taking care of the sick and wounded all the time."

"Ya pro'bly right, chile. With all da cookin', cleanin' and carin' we has to do fo all da young boys getting shot up, it sho does keep a body busy."

Katherine set a large pot on the stove and began dipping water into it. As she turned to dip grits out of a sack to put in the pot, Rosa suggested, "Let's feed'em oatmeal today. Them Bluecoats been fussing 'bout eatin' grits every day."

"I would think that if you're lying on your back and can't feed yourself, anything would taste good," Katherine responded as she dipped oatmeal from a sack. "Much better than anything they're getting when out in the mountain fighting, I reckon."

"Ya pro'bly right, chile. When is 'Lizabeth gonna get up?"

"I'm not sure," Katherine answered softly, not wanting to raise any suspicion on her roommate. She had heard Elizabeth creep into their room just a couple of hours before getting up that morning and figured she had stayed most of the night with the

Union officer. They usually worked as a team to help Rosa in the kitchen, rotating with other young girls from the boarding school who also stayed to help care for the wounded. But it looked like it was up to Katherine alone to help this morning.

Thomas came in through the back screen door with a basket of eggs just gathered from the henhouse and handed them to Katherine. "Got us a few double yolks today. Don't see many of them. Mus' be plenty fo them hens to eat."

Rosa handed him a couple of pails. "Here, Thomas, go milk them cows. I should have the feedin' done when ya gits back. Then we can eat."

"Yessum," Thomas replied as he turned to go back outside.

Rosa pulled two sheet pans of biscuits out of the oven as Katherine continued to stir the oatmeal pot. Sliding a knife under the biscuits so they wouldn't stick to the hot pan, Rosa asked, "Ya been back up to see that boy yet?"

Katherine glanced away, still stirring. "Yes, I went up last night to see him. I kinda felt bad about fussing with him about the war and all."

Rosa glanced toward Katherine, and asked, "Y'all still havin' words?"

She turned to face Rosa, wiping her hands on her apron, "No, not anymore. Doc Foster wants him to start walking some today. He asked me to take a walk with him."

Rosa laughed, clapping her hands. "Lawdy, chile, I knowd ya was a dressin' up for a reason. I shoulda kept you two apart. Lawdy mercy, too late now, I reckon."

"Morning, Rosa, Katherine," Elizabeth greeted them as she entered the kitchen.

"Morning, chile," Rosa replied. "You slow 'bout gittin' up this mornin'."

"Yes, I had trouble falling to sleep last night. Had a lot on my mind, I reckon," she said, glancing at Katherine to see her reaction. Katherine avoided her eyes.

Rosa looked at Elizabeth, "Chile, you feelin' all right? Ya look kinda pale this morning."

She averted her eyes while answering, "I'm fine; I just need to wake up."

Rosa watched from the corner of her eye. "Ya ain't losing sleep over one of these boys here, are ya? Having one of ya thinkin' 'bout courtin' is enough."

"I ain't a courting!" Katherine snapped. "I'm just going to walk with Sam to make sure he's okay. That's all."

"Whatever ya wants to call it." Rosa laughed, as Elizabeth sighed with relief.

With the food trays finally ready, Katherine, Elizabeth, and a couple of other girls began to take them to the rooms.

Katherine walked up three flights of stairs to Sam's room, stopping in the hallway foyer to look in the mirror hanging on the wall over the vanity table. Not satisfied with what she saw, she untied her long hair, letting it unravel and fall down across her shoulders. Picking up the tray, she stepped to the door and knocked.

"Come in," Sam called out.

He was sitting in a chair beside the bed that he had tried to make up. *Not bad, but still a few wrinkles*, Katherine thought as she entered. Sam was wearing his long-sleeve shirt unbuttoned, the bandages around his chest and right arm exposed as he lay back in the chair with his legs stretched out.

Katherine also noticed his clean-shaven face and how muscular and handsome he looked. "You trying to get an early start?" she asked, smiling as she moved closer.

"Doc was in here earlier and changed my bandages. Figured I would just get up, so I could start getting my strength back." He pushed himself up to a sitting position. "I can't do it lying in that bed."

"You did a lot of bleeding. It's gonna take you more than a couple of days to get your strength back. Maybe more like a couple of weeks."

"You're probably right. But I have to start trying. Today is as good a day as any, I reckon."

With the food tray on his lap, Katherine sat on the bed, watching him.

Spooning the oatmeal and picking up a biscuit, he asked, "How many wounded men are here now?"

"I think we have twelve here now. All the Bluecoats are downstairs. We're keeping you Confederates upstairs. We have more Bluecoats up the street at the Tavern. Trying to keep y'all separated so you won't be fussing and fighting with each other."

"I can't believe I'm in the same house with Bluecoats after what they done to me." Biting into a biscuit, he shook his head.

Watching him eat, Katherine realized with a little flutter in her heart that she was beginning to be attracted to this boy. It was a new feeling for her, but she liked the way it felt. She had to pull herself back from her thoughts to react to what he had said.

"Well, the hospital is off limits for any fighting. You can't have weapons in here. Sheriff Bradley sees to that."

Sam took a drink of milk, and then stared at Katherine. "I gotta get myself well so I can return to the militia. They need me."

"I'm sure they do. But let's just work on getting you well first. Let's take it one day at a time for the next couple of weeks. What do you think?"

Nodding his head, he agreed, "Fine with me."

"Good! I'm going down to help the other girls and Rosa in the kitchen. When you're ready to try to walk, let me know. I'll take a break and walk with you." She stood up to leave.

"Katherine..." Sam gazed at her with his dark-brown eyes that seemed to hold her in a trance. He held out his hand and said, "Thanks for helping take care of me and...and you look mighty pretty in that dress today. I want you to know that."

Katherine blushed, stifling the urge to reach for his hand. "Thank you, thank you, Sam," she said. There was a smile on her face as she walked away.

A couple of hours later, Sam, with a walking stick, and Katherine by his side, slowly and casually walked from the hospital down the main street in Abingdon.

"I don't see how these people live so close together," Sam pointed out. "Wonder how they make a living all boxed up in these houses?"

"Well, let's see," Katherine replied, counting off on her fingers. "We have a tinsmith who makes things like our forks and spoons, small tin canisters to hold our spices, trays, candleholders, and many things you find in a home. We have our blacksmith to tend to shoeing the horses and mending our wagon wheels. There's the weaving shop," Katherine pointed across the road. "He spins and dyes the thread for us to make our clothes and beddings. We have merchants selling us our shoes, foods we can't grow, hardware, and clothes from faraway places. Others here help run the railroad and Western Union."

Passing a well-dressed man with a beard, Katherine nodded and said, "Good morning, Mr. Lawson."

The man tipped his hat to her. "Morning to you, madam."

She whispered, "That's one of the lawyers who help run our courts here in Abingdon."

Shaking his head, Sam said, "Don't care much for them lawyers."

"Why not?" She turned toward him.

" 'Cause Pa said you can't trust 'em. He saw one stand in a courtroom one time swearin' to tell the truth. When he was called up to speak to the judge, everything he said was a lie."

"How did your pa know that?"

" 'Cause Pa overheard our neighbor when he was talking to the railroad man about sellin' his trestles to them. They agreed on a price and shook hands on it. When he got paid for the timbers, it wasn't the amount they agreed on. Our neighbor went to the court and filed a complaint against the railroad. When the railroad man came to court, he brought one of them dressed-up lawyers that represent the railroad. He stood up there and talked for ten minutes, Pa said. Judge threw it out of court, said it was his word against them."

Stopping and opening her hands, she said, "Why didn't your pa just say something?"

"He tried. Judge said he should have hired a lawyer and entered Pa as a witness. It was too late then."

"I guess I don't understand all that," she said as they began walking again.

"Pa says that lawyers are all we seem to be sending to Washington to represent us. He says that one day we won't have any rights anymore. We'll all be working for the government instead of them working for us. That's the reason I'm fighting in the militia. They have no right coming down here and taking away what we worked for. If they want something, they should have to work for it like we do."

A lady wearing a long, blue dress and matching bonnet walked out of a store that had a sign on it which read "Cheney's Cloth and Fabric Store."

"Morning, Miss Katherine," she said.

"Good morning, Mrs. Cheney." Noticing her staring at Sam, Katherine said, "This is Sam, one of the Confederate boys who has been recovering at the hospital."

"Morning, madam," Sam nodded.

The woman smiled and replied, "Glad to meet you, Sam." Turning her attention back to Katherine, she said, "Would you mind letting the girls over at the school or hospital know that Claude just got a new load of winter yarns and wool in? It's going to be our only order since it's hard to get deliveries because of the war."

"I'll let them know," Katherine said with a smile.

As she walked away, Katherine whispered, "That was Mrs. Cheney. She helps her husband run the business at their cloth store."

"Don't think I could get used to living in a town like this and staying all boxed up inside a store." He shook his head at the thought.

Katherine glanced up the street and saw several people whom she knew and thought it might be good if Sam met some of them. But before they could reach them, she saw a couple of Union soldiers on horseback riding toward them on their way to the hospital to check on their wounded soldiers. Afraid Sam might say something to them, she looked for a distraction.

"Sam, would you mind coming with me into this shop? I need some yarn so I can start making a winter sweater."

"Sure, wherever you want to go," Sam replied, following her into the store.

Once inside, a very colorful room greeted them. Rolls of cloth of many colors, reds, greens, blues, and more were stacked on a table to their right. Baskets with skeins of yarn, all stacked and leaning, were on the wall to their left. Behind the wooden counter on the back wall were pouches of needles for sewing, buttons of different sizes and colors, spools of thread, thimbles, and other sewing accessories. A potbellied stove sat in the corner where Mr. Cheney, a short man wearing glasses, sleeves rolled up, was busy unpacking crates of merchandise.

"Morning, Miss Katherine," he said, glancing up as she walked in.

"Good morning, Mr. Cheney. I'm looking for yarn today."

"These just came in and will possibly be the only yarn I can get this winter." He pointed to baskets against the wall. "Union won't let anything come through the ports, and rail service has all but stopped. Best get what you want before I run out."

Katherine picked up several skeins of yarn, then turned to Sam and asked, "What color do you like?"

Sam looked at the yarn and said, "I like that." He pointed at a golden auburn skein. "It matches the color of your hair."

"Then that's what I'll get." Back at the counter, she realized she had no money.

Mr. Cheney walked up. "Did you find what you needed?"

"Yes I did, but can you hold it for me? I'll come back and pay you later. I didn't bring money with me."

"Yes, that'll be fine, Katherine."

Sam stepped up. "Here, I'll pay for it." He tossed a coin onto the counter.

Katherine turned, protesting, "Sam, no, I don't want you to pay for it."

Sam smiled. "Least I can do for a pretty girl who's been taking care of me, I reckon."

Outside, Katherine asked, "Sam, where do you want to go now?"

"Reckon I need to go back to the hospital. I'm startin' to tire a little. Probably need to rest for a spell."

"Can you make it back walking?"

"Yes, but we need to move slowly. It kinda hurts when I breathe hard."

"Here, put your arm around my shoulder. Maybe it'll help take some of the weight off of you." Slowly, they walked back to the hospital.

Throughout the day as she worked, Katherine found herself purposely walking by the room to check on Sam whenever she had a chance. Several times, she glanced up from working to find Sam out of his room and watching her from a distance. No words were spoken, no gestures were made. Their eyes would simply meet.

Finally, at the end of the day, back in her room, Katherine reached for her diary and wrote:

Sam and I went for a walk today. I got to know him a little bit more. Seems to be honest and doesn't mind saying what he believes in.

Kept myself busy all day, but couldn't get Sam out of my mind. Maybe it's the way he talks or smiles at me, or maybe it's because he's so different from other boys. Hope he asks me to walk with him again.

CHAPTER 10
The First Fight

Katherine stood up and walked out from under the gazebo. Checking the time, Spencer realized it was noon and he had been sitting and listening to Katherine talk for two hours. Laying his laptop down, he stepped to the end of the gazebo and leaned against a post, watching her. He found himself entranced with the beauty of this young girl who walked so gracefully from bush to tree, touching the foliage, just as a child would discovering the sensation of touch for the first time. She seemed to illuminate everything around her. But somehow, at the same time, she seemed so out of place. Finally, she turned back toward him.

Spencer began thinking of how he might get Katherine up closer to the Inn, so someone else would see her. At least he could verify to everyone that she did exist. Maybe someone would know her, and he could find out what the motive was for Katherine's fascination with the past and this story she so passionately related. He thought, *Maybe I can get her to go with me to the patio table below the steps. I could keep writing and surely someone would see us up there, since it is the only entrance into the Inn from the pool.*

She walked back to the gazebo with a flower in her hand.

"Katherine, let's move up closer to the Inn. There's a table on the patio I can work on up there and the chairs would be more comfortable than these benches."

Spencer watched her caress each petal between her fingers.

"Yes, we could move closer to the porch. It looks like rain may come any time." She looked out into the still-lingering fog.

Spencer gathered his laptop, and they walked the sidewalk up towards the patio. A young boy and girl were walking toward them, holding hands. Spencer watched them closely to see their reaction as they approached.

The young girl's eyes were fixed on Katherine. When they came abreast, she stopped and said, "That's a beautiful dress. May I ask where you got it?"

Katherine stared blankly for a few seconds, as if surprised, then said, "Mama made it for me." She twirled the flower she held between her fingers.

The young couple stood close with the girl holding onto the arm of the young man, leaning on his shoulder. They continued to stand close while speaking.

"Well, it's absolutely beautiful. I've never seen one like it before. It's almost like something old-fashioned, or has that 'way back when' look. Does your mother make dresses to sell? May I?" She reached out and felt the material of Katherine's dress.

Katherine smiled. "No, Mama only makes them for me, my sisters, and herself. I've never known her to sell one."

The young girl frowned.

Spencer was delighted that he was watching Katherine have a conversation with someone else. He decided to join in. "Hello, my name is Spencer Aubreys," he said, as he held out his hand.

The young boy reached out his hand and they shook. "My name is Todd, and this is my fiancée, Judi. We're looking at the gazebo in the back lot and maybe want to have our wedding here next June."

"Then I guess congratulations are in order to both of you. This is Katherine Broadwater." He gestured toward her.

Katherine smiled and said, "Sam is coming home from the war this weekend. We can finally be together and I will be his wife." Her eyes sparkled.

"I know you must be really excited," Judi said. "I can only imagine how you feel to have the love of your life returning from service and starting your new life together."

"You must be the father of the bride?" Todd asked, looking at Spencer.

"No, I'm just a friend." Spencer smiled and shook his head at the thought. "I'm actually just visiting the Inn trying to get some inspiration for writing a book."

"I'm sure you will find inspiration here. This is a beautiful place with lots of history to write about. Spencer Aubreys, was it? I'll make a note of your name and watch for your book," Todd replied.

"Thanks for the encouragement."

Judi smiled at Katherine. "Tell your mama that she really knows how to make pretty dresses. And I know you'll have a beautiful wedding. I wish we could come by and see it. But we're traveling this weekend. Know that we wish you the best."

Katherine smiled.

"Good luck to you two," Spencer said. "I know you'll have a beautiful wedding."

"Good luck on your book, Mr. Aubreys," Todd said.

The young couple walked away, arms locked, leaning on each other.

Spencer and Katherine made their way up to the patio table set close to a wooden wall to the right of the steps. He was convinced that if anyone walked down and looked to their left, they could easily see him with Katherine.

He felt more at ease with the conversation they had with Todd and Judi and that someone else had actually seen and talked with Katherine. However, he still had suspicion as to what her intentions were for telling him this story. Also, he was trying to separate fact from fiction, hearing Katherine so convincingly speak about her plans to be reunited with Sam this weekend. Spencer watched as Katherine lifted the flower again to smell the blossom. It reminded him of her innocence, and he marveled at the beauty she radiated. Still, he had an unsatisfied curiosity gnawing at him. Maybe if he got her to finish her story, he would have answers to his questions.

"Did you and Sam spend more time together?" Spencer asked, his laptop open and ready to write.

Katherine gleamed and perked up, "I can't wait to see him. I'm just so excited."

"Yes, tell me more." Spencer began to write.

Sitting in rockers on the front porch, Sam and Katherine enjoyed each other's company on another hot August evening. Sam carved on a stick with an Old Timer pocketknife while Katherine knitted from the skein of yarn she had picked up several days earlier. They spent as much time together as they could while Sam continued to improve and regain his strength. Close friends now, they cherished their time together, often with humor, laughter and teasing.

Sam leaned back in his rocker. "You know, being around you this past week has kinda made me forget the war's goin' on."

Katherine smiled as she continued knitting. "You need to have something to think about instead of just fighting all the time."

"Yeah, you're probably right. I hope the war ends soon. I need to get back home and help Pa and Joe. I know they're worried about me."

Looking at Sam, she questioned him, "Why go back out and fight? Why not just go back home?"

"I would like to. But I wouldn't have peace of mind if I quit. Too many men countin' on me. Got to do my part."

Suddenly, two Union soldiers rode up and stopped in front of the hospital. They dismounted and stepped onto the porch. Looking at Katherine, then Sam, they gave him a disapproving glance before entering the hospital.

Standing up and putting his knife away, Sam leaned against a porch column and turned to Katherine. "Do you have a fella waitin' for you somewhere?"

"No, I don't," she said, shaking her head. "Never met one I was interested in. Besides, I've been busy trying to get my schooling until the war put a stop to that."

"Yeah, the war's changed plenty for everyone." Glancing away, he asked, "When it's over, can I come back to see you?"

Not wanting to sound too anxious, Katherine sighed and smiled. "Sure, Sam. I was hoping you would come back to see me."

"After all the caring you've done for me, it's the least I can do."

The two Union soldiers stepped back out onto the porch. One of them lifted his hat and said, "Evenin', Ma'am. Hope to see you around again."

Katherine didn't reply as the Union soldier eyed Sam before walking away. Sam's frown was intense.

Then Rosa walked out onto the porch. "I wondered where ya young'uns were," she said. "Katherine, it's 'bout time to start supper. But first I need to send some clean bandaging cloths up to the Tavern. Do ya mind takin' some up there fo me?"

Katherine stood and rolled her knitting into a bundle. "Sure, I'll do it."

Sam stepped away from the porch column. "I'll walk with you."

Rosa went into the house and returned with an armful of clean cloths. Sam and Katherine each took a bundle and began walking up the street, deserted except for several horses and buggies parked in front of the shops.

"Does it get this quiet every evening out here?" Sam asked.

"Townsfolk like to get their business done before it gets late. Everyone's scared what the Union may decide to do."

"They don't have any reason to pick on you."

"No, but if they knew we had a militia here aiding the Confederates, they would probably raid Abingdon. Those two Bluecoats that just left the hospital were Union officers checking on their wounded back there. They come in every few days."

"I think one of them has an eye on you."

"Won't do him no good. I'm not taking to liking any Bluecoat. I know what they've been doing to folks here in the South." Katherine spoke firmer, shaking her head as they walked.

Just then, she heard someone call to her. She glanced across the street and saw Sheriff Bradley approaching them.

"Good evening, Katherine," he said, tipping his hat to her and nodding at Sam as he stopped to greet them. "Glad to see you're up and about, son. You didn't look so good when they first brought you in."

"I'm doing much better." He smiled toward Katherine. "Had some good folks takin' care of me."

"Are you going back to join the militia?"

"Yes, word's out that they're sending for us and want to get us out by the weekend."

"I want you to know that Abingdon is behind you. We just can't show it. With all these Bluecoats hangin' around, it's got everybody nervous. It's like we're sitting on a powder keg that's about to go off. Wouldn't take much for us to find ourselves in the middle of this war."

"I hope not. You've got a pretty town here."

"Let's hope it stays that way. I am making my rounds, so I'll see you two later. Enjoy the evening and good luck, Sam," he added as he walked away.

Continuing toward the Tavern, Katherine asked, "Are you looking forward to going back and joining the Confederates?"

"At first I was, but now I'm kinda dreading it. You were right; a man needs something to think about besides fightin'. Don't mind leaving Abingdon, but not seeing you will be the hard part."

"I'm gonna miss you, too." Katherine smiled.

As they neared the Tavern, Katherine noticed the two horses tied outside that the Union officers had ridden on earlier. She knew the officers were inside checking on their wounded men.

Not wanting Sam to go in, she turned to him and said, "You wait outside for me. I'll take these bandages in and be right back out."

"I don't mind goin' in. It's just a bunch of Bluecoats in there. I won't start any trouble."

Katherine implored again, "Sam, please."

He handed her the bandages. "Okay, but if you need me, just holler. I'll stand to the side of the building."

Katherine went to the door. With one last look at Sam, she entered. Three Bluecoats, sitting at a table talking, eyed her closely, as she walked to the back room. She found an older lady and two young girls cleaning up.

"Here are the clean bandages Rosa sent," she said.

The older lady said, "Thanks for bringing them up. We were almost out. Seems like we gettin' more wounded boys in here every week. We've got the hospital and the Tavern full now. Don't have room for any more."

Katherine reminded them, "The fighting is getting closer to town all the time. Sheriff says we're sitting on a powder keg about to go off."

Grinning, one of the younger girls said, "Word's gettin' 'round that one of the Bluecoats down at the hospital is taking a likin' to Elizabeth."

Not wanting to say anything negative to reflect on Elizabeth, she replied, "Maybe he'll be gone soon. I hope so for her sake." She backed away. "I need to get on back and help Rosa with supper."

As Katherine walked through the front room, one of the Union officers stood up and blocked her path. "Mighty nice of you to follow us up here to see me again."

Katherine stared at him sharply, "I didn't follow you anywhere. I brought bandages that were needed," she answered, sticking her chin out.

Smiling snidely, he continued, "Well, since you're here, why not sit down with us so's we can have us a chance to get acquainted?"

She returned his smile with a scowl. "Reckon I don't need to be wastin' my time." She took a step backward.

"You know, I kind of like that. You got a little spunk in you. Must be your red hair."

As Katherine tried to step around him, he grabbed her by the arm and pulled her to the table, forcing her down onto his lap. "Now all I'm asking for is a little conversation for a few minutes. That ain't gonna hurt you, is it?"

"Let me go!" Katherine screamed as she slapped him and pushed away, trying to break free.

Struggling to hold her down, he said, "Boys, I do believe we done got us a feisty one here."

"Let her go!" Sam stood inside the door, his fist clenched, and a stern look on his face.

"Well, now, who is this?" the officer sneered. Looking surprised, but still holding Katherine down, the Bluecoat said, "Is this your bodyguard? Boy, you better take yourself back to the hospital and find yourself a front porch rocking chair. You gonna be messing with real men up here, who's too much for you."

"When a girl says no around here, she means no," Sam declared, not flinching.

Glancing at the other two Bluecoats who were leaning forward menacingly, one turned to Sam. "What do you intend to do about it, boy? It's three of us and one of you."

"I done asked you once. Next time won't be so good for you."

"Well, I see today you gonna learn a lesson, boy. You southern boys just don't know when you're whupped, do you?" He pushed Katherine to the side and stood up.

In two swift steps, Sam was in his face. Catching the Bluecoat by surprise, he landed two swift jabs to his face, knocking him over the table. The other two Bluecoats charged at him. He kicked one in the gut, sending him reeling backwards. The other one grabbed

Sam and pushed him back against the wall. After struggling for a few seconds, Sam backed him from the wall and punched him in the gut, causing him to bend over. Then he kicked him in the face.

The girls in the back room ran out into the street screaming for help. Katherine stood firm, trying to figure out what she needed to do to help Sam.

Finally, the three Bluecoats regained their footing and charged Sam all at once, throwing him back against the wall. Two of them pinned his body and held his arms as the third Bluecoat threw a couple of punches into his gut and face. He groaned, struggling to breathe.

Sam mustered all his strength and kicked the Bluecoat in the chest, sending him reeling over the table again. Now weakened, Sam gasped for air but couldn't break loose from the two men holding him. Dazed, the Bluecoat lifted himself up off the floor and pulled a knife out of its holster. "Like I said, boy, today I'm gonna teach you southerners not to mess with us Union men," he said, moving toward Sam with a menacing grin.

Katherine ran up behind him, and he shoved her aside with one hand. Then she grabbed a chair and raised it with all her might to smash it over his head. But he wrested the chair from her then punched her in the face, knocking her to the floor. He turned, ready to stab Sam, when the click of a gun got his attention.

"Drop that knife or die!"

Glancing around, the Bluecoat saw Sheriff Bradley pointing a revolver at him. He placed the knife at Sam's throat and said, "Sheriff, it's three of us and you'll likely only get one shot off before we get you."

"One shot is all I need to put you down. Then we even the count, don't we? It's your move, soldier." He stared the Bluecoat in the eyes, not backing down.

The Bluecoat paused, and then released Sam from his grip. "We were just trying to scare him a little. He came in here and jumped us for no reason at all. You ain't taking sides against the Union, are you, Sheriff?"

Sam staggered over to help Katherine up from the floor.

"Maybe we just need to come in and burn this town down," the officer threatened.

Still holding his revolver at the ready, the Sheriff said, "I would advise you not to try that. After all, we're taking care of your wounded, aren't we? If you boys have differences, you settle them on the battlefield, not here."

Sheriff Bradley backed up a little and motioned with his gun. "Sam, Katherine, y'all get on outa here." Looking back at the Bluecoats, he said, "Now, boys, I'm not gonna lock you up this time. But if you start anymore trouble, I will. Doesn't matter whose uniform you're wearing. You're supposed to be here checking up on your wounded men. My advice to you is to get your business done and get out of town."

"Of course, Sheriff, we understand," the Bluecoat said.

"Now," Sheriff Bradley added, "I am backing out this door. I don't want you following me or these kids. I got people watching my back. Understand?"

"We understand. But the Union won't like the way we're getting treated. Remember that we warned you," the Bluecoat said with a smirk on his face.

Outside, Sheriff Bradley asked Katherine, "Can you two make it down to the hospital okay? I'll stand across the street and make sure they don't follow."

"I think we can make it." She had Sam's arm draped over her shoulder. Together they slowly walked away, holding each other for support.

Back at the hospital, Sam lay down on his bed, as Katherine unbuttoned his shirt to examine his chest while waiting for Doc Foster to come and check on him.

Doc Foster finally came in, mumbling, shaking his head. "Boy, you should at least wait until your ribs are healed before fighting." He pressed on his rib cage while asking him questions.

"You're lucky, son. Appeared they only hit you in your gut. If they had hit you higher, it would've broken those fractured ribs.

You'll have a bit of bruising. Take it easy over the next couple of days and you should be okay."

He turned and frowned at Katherine. "You need to put some cold cloths on your face. Looks like you're going to have a bit of bruising, also."

Before leaving he said, "You two ought to stay out of sight for a while. They're liable to come looking for you sooner or later. They know they can do whatever they want to and get away with it. I'll be downstairs if you need me."

Katherine and Sam stared at each other, hurting with bruised and battered faces, both searching for words to say to give each other comfort.

Finally, managing a smile, Sam said, "Looks like we had our first fight, didn't we?"

Trying to force a smile, holding a cold cloth to her face that was already swelling, Katherine said, "Yes, I think you're right, Sam, we did."

They both laughed, even though it hurt.

CHAPTER 11
Bonding

It was early Friday morning as Katherine and Elizabeth got ready to help Rosa with breakfast. Glancing in the mirror, Katherine tied her hair back and looked to see if the bruising on her face from the fight three days earlier had gotten lighter. Carefully, she touched the bruises still visible and tender on her face.

Watching her, Elizabeth said, "You have taken a liking to that Confederate boy, haven't you?"

Straightening her dress on her shoulders and glancing at Elizabeth through the mirror, Katherine said, "We've just become close friends. He's nice and has good manners, even if he doesn't have much schooling. Hope after the war we can still see each other."

"The Union officer I've been tending to wants me to leave with him tomorrow," Elizabeth said quietly, glancing away from Katherine.

Katherine turned to Elizabeth, dropping her hands open. "Why would he want you to leave with him, and where are you going?"

"He wants me to go with him back to Pittsburgh, Pennsylvania. That's where he's from." Elizabeth avoided eye contact.

Katherine paused. "Is he going to marry you?"

"We haven't talked about that. I suppose if I leave with him, he'd be planning to ask me." She picked clothes up from the bed to put away, still avoiding eye contact with Katherine.

Katherine placed her hands on her hips and stepped closer, making Elizabeth look up at her. "Elizabeth, you need to think about what you're doing and what you're about to give up. What about your family, your friends, and schooling?"

"After the war, there won't be any town or school to go to around here." She turned away to put the clothes in a drawer.

"How do you know that? What's going to happen?" Katherine spoke firmer.

" 'Cause he said the Union was going to win the war and they're going to have to burn Abingdon down anyway."

Katherine shook her head. "I don't understand. Why would they do that? We haven't done anything to them."

Elizabeth walked over to the dresser and began brushing her hair. Looking in the mirror back at Katherine, she said, "Something about Abingdon could be a supply route from the south. They think we're bootlegging supplies to the Confederates from the south to northern Virginia through Abingdon and Damascus."

Feeling sorry for her, Katherine realized that Elizabeth was probably being used. And what would her pa do if he knew she was planning to run off with a Bluecoat? She needed to talk her out of it, but waited for Elizabeth to turn around.

"Elizabeth, I know it's none of my business, but think about what you're doing. What would your pa do if he found out?"

She shrugged her shoulders, walking past Katherine. "Pa won't know until I'm gone. When the war's over, I'll come back home and visit. It won't make any difference then."

Katherine folded her arms and leaned against the wall and spoke softly, "Elizabeth, you've only known this man for a little over three weeks. You don't know enough about him to be leaving with him."

Angrily, Elizabeth snapped back, "You've only known Sam for two weeks and you love him! You don't have to say anything. It shows every time you two are together. You spend all your free time with him. All the girls here talk about you and him."

Biting her lip, Katherine pleaded with her, "Elizabeth, you don't understand what you're getting yourself into."

"Understand! Can't I love somebody?" She pointed her finger at her and shouted, "All you girls are jealous of me. You can't have what I have and it's getting to you!"

Backing away, Katherine held up her hands. "Okay, Elizabeth, I'm done talking to you. But please think about this before you do it. Let's go help Rosa. I know she needs us."

In the kitchen, Rosa was singing and rolling dough for biscuits. Thomas was adding wood to the stove to get it hot enough for cooking.

"Morning, young'uns," Rosa greeted them.

"Morning, Rosa, Thomas," Katherine replied.

"Katherine, you put de apples on and start de water for da oatmeal. 'Lizabeth, you can put de eggs in the boiling pot and start slicin' de side meat to fry."

As they began to work, Rosa asked, "What're ya two doin' today? It's Friday, and ya have most of the day off."

"I'm going to play my violin for the Bluecoats," Elizabeth replied. "The officer I've been caring for likes showing me off to the other Union men. Some officers are coming in this evening to make plans to move their wounded men out of here this weekend. He's leaving tomorrow." She cut her eyes at Katherine, hoping she wouldn't say anything about their earlier conversation.

"How 'bout you, Katherine?"

"Sam and I are going to get a couple of horses, ride out of town, and maybe do a picnic. We don't think it's a good idea for us to stay around town, since we've been fighting with those Union men earlier this week."

"Well, y'all enjoys yo free time. But be careful. Lots a talk goin' on 'bout the Bluecoats sending mo men down here to fight. People gettin' real scairt 'round here." Looking over at Thomas, she asked, "Ya wants to go fetch the eggs and milk the heifers?"

Thomas picked up a couple of pails and left.

Finally, after everyone at the hospital was fed, and the cleanup in the kitchen was done, Katherine took off her apron to check on Sam.

She knocked on the door and heard, "Come in."

She found Sam fully dressed, staring out the window with his arms crossed. "Good morning, Katherine. I've been thinking about you."

"I've been thinking about you too, Sam," Katherine replied, uncertainly shifting from one foot to another.

He continued to stare out the window. "I'm gonna have to be leavin' here tomorrow. The militia is gonna take us back to Damascus where we'll regroup and go back out to fight."

"I know what you have to do, Sam, and I understand why you're doing it." She stood in the center of the room, her hands clasped in front of her.

Gazing out the window, Sam stood silent, then turned and stepped toward her. Without saying a word, he extended his open palms to her. Slowly, Katherine, staring into his eyes, lifted her hands to his. Pulling her close, Sam reached up and untied her hair, letting it fall. Caressing her long hair with his fingers, moving closer, he rubbed it against his cheek. Placing his cheek against her face, his lips moved to her forehead, down to her cheek and then to her lips. Embracing each other, Sam's arms encircled her as Katherine's hands clasped his neck. They held each other for several moments without speaking.

Finally, Sam stepped back. Holding her hands and looking into her eyes, he spoke. "Katherine, I'm sorry, but I have no choice."

Lifting her finger to his lips, Katherine said. "I know what you have to do tomorrow, Sam. Let's just make today special so it will be ours to have and hold onto, today, tomorrow and forever." She swallowed hard, her voice quaking. "Let's not ruin it by talking about what has to happen tomorrow. Okay?" She glanced away and wiped a tear from her cheek.

"Katherine Broadwater," Sam squeezed her hand. "How much do you love me?"

"With all of me, Sam." She turned her gaze to his eyes. "All of me loves you." Sam sighed and said in a rush, "Katherine, I'm not sure how a man goes about saying this, but the last two weeks here with you have made me feel wanted in a way I've never felt before. Reckon I don't know exactly how a man's supposed to feel when he loves a woman, but I can't get you off my mind. I think of you when gettin' up every morning, and you're the last thing on my mind when I go to bed. Because of you I have more to look forward to than I've ever had. I don't ever want to lose this feeling. And I don't ever want to spend another day without knowing you're here with me."

Katherine pressed her lips together to keep them from quivering. "What are you trying to say?"

Sam reached and held her face with his fingers. He stared into her blue eyes, paused, then said, "Katherine Broadwater, I love you and want you to be my wife."

Katherine inhaled deeply and searched for words to say, but found herself unable to speak as tears rolled down her cheeks.

Sam pulled her close, her head resting against his chest with his face buried in her hair. They stood silent for several minutes.

Finally, Katherine looked up at him, crying and smiling, then said, "Yes, Sam, I'll be your wife."

Sam sat her down on the bed, and then sat in the bedside chair in front of her. Holding her hands, he said, "I have no choice but to go back out and fight. But by winter I will come back home for you. I know this is kinda fast but I want us to marry today if we can."

"Oh," Katherine said, dropping her gaze down to their hands. That was a lot sooner than she had thought. She wouldn't have time to plan the wedding she had always dreamed of. But she loved Sam, and she knew that with the war on, lots of people had gotten married before the men went off to war. But Mama and Papa...

She looked back up. "But Mama and Papa won't have time to get here to see us get married."

"I want us to have us a big wedding, too," Sam declared. "I want Pa and Joe here, but I want to know before I leave again that you will be here waiting for me when I get back. So let's get married today but not tell anybody until I come back home. Then we will have us a big wedding party with all the kinfolk and tell them that we are married."

Katherine's eyebrows rose with a twinkle in her eyes, "Yes, Sam, I reckon we can. But if we get us a preacher, then everyone will know."

"I've thought about that. Let's get Judge Grey to marry us. He can do it. We'll tell him we're not telling anyone until I come back home. Then we'll have us a big wedding party with all the fixin's and folks can do a pounding for us then."

"But my name will change and folks will know I'm married," Katherine said, looking at him questionably.

Holding her hands, Sam stood and pulled her close to him. "Katherine, I love you and want you to be my wife. Once we're married, reckon it won't do no harm if you still keep your name for a while. This way it stays our secret until I come home for you and then we can change your name."

Katherine pressed her lips tight, thinking, then smiled and said, "Yes, Sam, I reckon we could."

They stood holding onto each other, gazing into each other's eyes and beaming, thinking about the plans that were unfolding before them.

Finally, Katherine stepped back, her voice quivering, and said, "I need to go finish my chores or we won't have any time together."

"Then I will go find the judge to let him know and get the horses ready for us to ride out."

"I'll fix us a picnic lunch." Stepping back, her hands slipped from Sam's grasp.

"I'll be on the porch waiting when you're ready."

"I'll hurry. I will hurry real fast, Sam," she said, then turned and left the room.

On the way to the kitchen, Katherine met Elizabeth in the hallway. Neither had spoken since their argument earlier that morning.

She stopped her and spoke softly. "Elizabeth, maybe I was wrong when I spoke to you this morning. It's not for me to decide how much you love someone or what you're going to do about it. Just know that I was concerned for you. I wish you the best whatever you decide to do."

"I wish the best for you, too," Elizabeth said as she stepped forward and gave Katherine a hug. "When I go away, let's promise to write each other and stay in touch."

"Certainly," Katherine said.

"I hope it works out for you and Sam, too," Elizabeth said.

"I'm sure it will," she said, glancing away. "Take care of yourself now."

Katherine watched Elizabeth walk away, wishing she could tell her of their plans to get married that day.

CHAPTER 12

Forever

An hour later, Sam stood on the porch talking to Sheriff Bradley. "I want to thank you, Sheriff, for saving me from those Bluecoats at the Tavern. I could've whupped them if I didn't have these fractured ribs."

Sheriff Bradley leaned against a post, swiping his hat at a yellow jacket flying around. "No doubt you would've beat 'em. They just don't fight fair. Putting those blue uniforms on makes those boys think they can do what they want and get by with it."

Sam spoke, as Sheriff Bradley only made the insect more aggressive. "I'll have my chance at 'em on the battlefield, I reckon. I want to hurry and get the war over so I can come back to Abingdon."

"I just hope it's still standing then." Finally the sheriff knocked the yellow jacket out of the air to the porch. "Talk goin' 'round they're thinking 'bout burning us down."

"Do you have enough men in the militia to stop 'em?"

Sheriff Bradley stepped forward to where the insect landed. "Not a whole unit, but I got a few men watching 'em closely." He stepped on the creature, crushing it. "We're ready if they want to try."

Katherine came out to the porch with her hands behind her; she nodded at Sheriff Bradley.

Sheriff Bradley said, "I gotta make my rounds. You kids be careful today."

"Yes, Sheriff, we will," Sam replied, never taking his eyes off Katherine. Her hair cascaded across her shoulders and shone so brightly that it illuminated the spot where she stood.

"Close your eyes, Sam!" she said with a twinkle in her eyes.

Closing his eyes, he felt something soft being put around his neck. Reaching up, he caught her hands. Opening his eyes, he saw a knitted scarf made from the yarn he had bought for her several days earlier.

"I thought you were going to make yourself a sweater." He reached for it and rubbed it between his fingers.

Katherine clasped her hands together, pleased that Sam liked it. "I'll have plenty of time for that. I just want you to have something to take with you so you'll remember me while you're away."

Sam chuckled. "I won't have any trouble thinkin' about you. I ain't gone yet, and I already can't wait to be coming back." He reached and touched her cheek.

Katherine laughed. "Let's get going or we're going to be missing our day together."

They walked down to the hitching post.

"Judge Grey is gonna meet us on the footpath just outside of town. He's gonna marry us, and then we can be on our way," Sam said. He helped Katherine mount her horse and then he mounted his. They rode down toward the footpath. After riding a ways they came upon Judge Grey standing by his horse.

"Are you sure you want to do this?" he asked, looking back and forth at each of them.

"We're sure," they said simultaneously, making all three laugh at the same time.

They walked up on a hillside with a view of ridges and grassy meadows, the judge leading the way and Sam and Katherine following, holding hands and stealing glances at each other.

"This is as good a place as any, I reckon," Judge Grey said.

Turning around, he looked at Katherine and asked, "Miss Katherine, you know you've only known each other a short time."

Katherine looked at Sam, and then said evenly, "Yes, I know. And I know I want to be his wife."

Judge Grey stared at Sam and spoke firmly, "Son, she's one of ours. I've known this young lady and her family most her life.

We're not gonna take it lightly now if you make her unhappy. Your intentions better be good, and you better take care of her."

"I'm gonna take care of her." Sam took Katherine's hands. "I'm gonna take care of you and love you forever, I promise," he said gazing into her eyes.

"Then I guess the only thing that's left for me to do is get you two married," the judge said. "I've never been one to stand in the way of love."

Holding up a Bible, Judge Grey began to recite the words that would bind Katherine and Sam as husband and wife. A gentle breeze blew as Katherine leaned against Sam and held onto his sweaty hand. A perfect moment of peace and tranquility unfolded, embracing their overwhelming love for one another as Judge Grey spoke the words they longed to hear.

"By the power vested to me by this great Confederate State of Virginia and town of Abingdon, I hereby declare you husband and wife." He paused and then said, "You may kiss your bride or whatever you're supposed to do now," purposely glancing away

After Katherine and Sam stepped back from each other, Judge Grey said, "I guess congratulations are in order to both of you. Katherine, I will have the marriage certificate locked in the safe at the courthouse. Come by and get it, and I won't say anything to anyone until you decide to tell them." He shook Sam's hand. "Good luck to you, son. We hope to have you back at home with us soon. You two enjoy your time together, but be careful. There are Bluecoats swarming around everywhere and more showing up down here every day."

Judge Grey rode off as Sam and Katherine went in the opposite direction. Awhile later they came to an open grassy meadow high on a ridge where they could look out and see for miles. Once the horses were tied, Sam spread a blanket on the grassy hilltop. Katherine got a saddle pouch from her horse and took food from it. They arranged the food on the blanket, then looking shyly at each other, sat down and began to fill their plates.

While they ate, Sam reminisced about his home town. "When the war's over, I been thinkin' 'bout gettin' Pa to give me a piece of land so I can build a house on it. We have high mountains and ridges just like this. I know the perfect spot to build us a house on." Sam paused, watching Katherine's reaction.

"I bet you would build a beautiful house," she said.

"Are you up to leavin' Abingdon? I thought we could make our home in Galax, next to Pa's home place."

"Yes, Sam. I will go with you most anywhere."

Sam lay back on the blanket, his hands under his head and stared up at the sky, a smile on his face.

"Here's dessert," Katherine said. "Rosa gave me some of her dried apples, so I made us some fried apple pies."

"Mighty nice of her," Sam said as he reached for one.

For hours, Sam and Katherine talked, laughed and shared more of their lives with one another, both trying to forget about the journey he would have to make the next day. Finally, the conversation ended, they held hands and stared into each other's eyes. Sam reached over and caressed her face ever so gently, as though he thought if he pressed too hard she would break. With her hair brushing his hands, he pulled her close and they began to kiss passionately.

In his arms, Katherine felt warm and aroused in a way that she had never known. Sam's hand moved from her face to her breast. Instinctively, Katherine reached to stop him, so he dropped his hand from her. Breathing heavily, she tried to speak but couldn't find the words she wanted to say.

Sam continued to kiss her with one hand tangled in her hair, while she held his other. With her heart racing and body trembling, she savored the feelings that began to unfold within her. Not knowing what was expected of her, but yearning for his touch, all Katherine could think about was loving Sam.

Sliding to the ground they began to let the desire they had for each other unfold and engulf them. Sam's hands began to explore her body, followed by kisses, then slowly removing their clothes.

Finally, they lay in each other's arms, trembling and molded together, both giving and receiving all they had, until their passion subsided.

Afterwards, in each other's arms, they said nothing as a gentle breeze caressed them. The only sound they heard was each other's breathing, as they lay savoring the moment.

Finally, after dressing, Sam sat up, holding Katherine in his arms. He held her hand with his left hand and caressed her hair with the other. Finally speaking, Sam said, "Katherine, I didn't mean for this to happen for you like this, on top of a mountain in the middle of nowhere."

Katherine glanced up, her face flushed and eyes twinkling. "Sam, I don't want you to apologize for loving me. Maybe someday…" she swallowed, "…it won't have to be like this for us."

Sitting her upright, Sam reached for both of her hands. "I know we won't have but one night together before I have to leave. Judge Grey said we could use his home place outside of town tonight if we want some time together for ourselves. I will slip you out once it gets dark tonight so no one will know we're gone. But I promise, once I get back this winter, we're going to find us a fine place to go to."

"I want more for us, too, Sam. But I know what the war is doing to folks, and I know you have to go back out and fight." She glanced away, not wanting him to see tears welling in her eyes. "If this is all the time we can have for now, then I will cherish these two weeks until we can be together again. Okay?" She sniffled.

Hours passed, filled with talk and plans of what their lives would be like once they could be together forever…their home in Galax, Katherine finishing her schooling, a house full of kids and a family business were dreams painted with words. Watching and listening to each other, their eyes gazed and hands caressed one another. The only moment in time they knew was the one they now shared.

Suddenly, cannon and gunfire erupted from one of the many ridges that surrounded them. Startled, Sam stood up and looked around, trying to figure out where the noise came from. "There must be a fight goin' on a ways from here. We best head back to town and find out what's goin' on."

Sam helped Katherine to her feet. They rolled the blanket and packed everything back on their horses and galloped back toward Abingdon. Neither said a word, riding side by side, trying to hide the worry they had for what might await them in town.

After almost an hour of riding, while the gunfire continued around them, they knew battles were raging close by. Finally, making their way back to the footpath, they walked the horses from the trail to the horse stable.

They were met by Thomas and Judge Grey. Both looked nervous and frightened.

Thomas ran up to Katherine, "Miss Katherine, sumpin' terrible done happened!"

"What is it, Thomas?" she asked.

"We've got trouble," Judge Grey said, stepping up and taking Katherine's reins. "Elizabeth's dad came over to the hospital and killed the Union officer who was staying there. He came in raving about how no Bluecoat was gonna defile his daughter. Took his gun and shot him. The officer didn't even have a weapon on him."

Katherine stepped from her horse, suddenly shaking and pale. "What about Elizabeth, is she all right?"

"She left with some of the townsfolk. The Bluecoats are out looking for her dad. Sheriff Bradley is trying to convince them that it wasn't an act of war, but just an individual act of rage by her dad. God help him if they catch him. There are skirmishes already going on all around us. Also, we heard they're planning a raid in Abingdon to arrest all the Confederates here at the hospital," Judge Grey nervously reported.

"What do we need to do?" asked Sam.

"We have six men—and now you—ready to get y'all out of town before they get here. The others are hidden in the caves under Abingdon and should be here in a minute. We'll get y'all back to Damascus by way of the footpath. We've got horses saddled and ready for you in the stable and want to get y'all out of here while there's light for you to travel."

Katherine tried hard not to show any emotion, wanting to be strong for Sam, knowing now they wouldn't have anymore time together. Sam stepped over to her side and, without saying a word, he took her hand and held it.

Seven men approached from the stable. Katherine recognized one to be the Confederate officer who had ridden up and talked to Judge Grey and Sheriff Bradley almost two weeks before.

"We best be movin' out," the officer said. "The fewer of us around when the Bluecoats get here, the better off this town will be."

"I hope you're right," Judge Grey agreed.

Katherine noticed how sweaty Sam's hands had become and searched for words to say, but words escaped her. She ran over to the horse he had been riding, got the knitted scarf, and brought it back to him. Speechless, Sam reached for her face with both hands, leaned over, and kissed her gently. His eyes teared up, and he cleared his throat.

"Sam, promise me…" She choked back tears, gazing into his eyes. "Promise me you'll come back."

Sam held her face only inches from his. "I promise I'll come back for you. I'll come back, and we can be together forever. I promise, Katherine."

Eight horses were brought from the stable, and the officer commanded, "Okay, men, time to mount up. We're leaving."

Holding onto his wrist tightly, Katherine pleaded, "Sam, you take care of yourself now, take care of yourself for me."

"I will, Katherine, I will." With a brush of his fingers to her cheek, he wiped her tears away. "I love you, Katherine Broadwater. I'll love you forever. I promise."

Composing himself, he turned away, mounted his horse, his face showing no expression.

Katherine forced a smile, then waved farewell.

Suddenly a young boy came running up and shouted, "There's a brigade of about twenty Bluecoats headed down the street toward the hospital!"

The officer looked back and shouted, "Okay, men, move out! Now!"

Holding her breath, Katherine felt every heartbeat, as her body tensed, trying to come to terms with Sam leaving. She watched, her heart breaking, as he and the other riders disappeared into the trees.

Her thoughts turned to the other girls at the hospital who might need her help, and she turned to walk back to the hospital. There she found Rosa and several of the girls standing on the back porch, crying and holding each other as the Bluecoats stormed the hospital.

Rosa stepped off the porch to meet Katherine. "Chile, I'm glad you is back. I was worried 'bout ya."

Katherine embraced Rosa, then broke down and began crying.

"What's wrong, chile?" Rosa asked softly.

"Sam had to leave. He said he loves me, and I love him."

Patting her back, Rosa replied, "I understan', chile, I understan'."

The shock of what had happened at the hospital and the Bluecoats' storming in and threatening to burn down the town had everyone on edge. Katherine continued to do what she could or was asked to do, but in somewhat of a daze, as all she could think about was Sam and wondering where he was and if he were safe.

Finally, late that night when the lanterns were turned down, Katherine returned to her room, which felt empty without Elizabeth. Sitting for a moment, thinking and feeling overwhelmed, she reached for her diary and began to write:

Today is the happiest and saddest day of my life. My heart hurts for Elizabeth. Maybe I should have tried to reason with her more about her fascination with the Union officer. Her pa killed him today.

Sam and I got married today. Judge Grey married us in an open meadow on top of a ridge outside of town. We won't tell anyone until he comes back home. Then we will have us a wedding party with our kinfolk. It's only been hours since he left to go join the fight, but I miss him so much my heart aches.

I now know what it's like to love and be loved by a man. Today I became a woman. Mama was right. It wasn't something that I could plan for. It just happened. I know I'll count the hours and days until Sam returns. I love you, Sam. All of me loves you.

CHAPTER 13
Waiting For Sam

Hours, days, and weeks passed as the Civil War continued to burden everyone's life in Abingdon. Merchants had trouble getting goods because the Union continued to attack the Confederate supply routes in Damascus and near Abingdon. They also tried cutting off supplies moving to northern Virginia. Men and boys, both Union and Confederate, wounded from battle, continued to be brought to the hospital. Katherine always rushed to see if Sam was among them. With no way to get a letter to or from him, and not knowing where he was, all she could do was hope and wait.

Doing what was expected of her, Katherine worked from daylight until dark just to keep her mind busy while hanging onto the dream of what life for her and Sam would be like once he returned. Longing for Sam filled every moment of her day now that she knew how it felt to love and be loved by a man.

Now she had a secret that she couldn't share with anyone yet. She longed to be able to tell Sam that, even though they had been together only once, they had been blessed with a child. Keeping the secret was making it even harder to be away from Sam. Often, she lay awake at night crying, longing to share with someone her secret about the new life that grew in her womb.

One late October evening, Katherine sat in a rocking chair on the back porch knitting a sweater from the yarn she had used to make Sam's scarf.

Rosa came to sit beside her and began to shell a basket of October beans. "Katherine, ya seem to have a lot on yo mind. What's troublin' ya?"

She knew she could trust Rosa, so she sat back, sighed, and tried to find the proper words. "I miss Sam something terrible. All I think about is him. The hurtin' I feel because he's not here has become unbearable. I don't know what to do."

"I understan', chile," Rosa said with a laugh. "I bet he's sittin' somewhere thinkin' about ya and feelin' the same way. Y'all will have plenty of time together."

Katherine dropped her eyes, paused and then said, "Rosa, Sam and I slipped away and got married before he left."

Rosa's eyes widened, and her mouth dropped open. "Why ain'tcha told us, chile?"

"We wanted to keep it a secret until he comes back from the war. He's coming back by winter, then we can have our families here and let everyone know and have us a wedding party."

"Mercy, chile, ya always full of susprises," Rosa chuckled, shaking her head.

"I'm with child," Katherine said quietly. "I'm going to have Sam's baby." She began crying.

Rosa stopped shelling beans, reached for Katherine's hand and glanced around to see if anyone was near. She spoke softly. "Why didn'tcha tell me, chile?" She paused. "Have ya told anyone else?"

"No, I can't, Rosa. You know what people would say and think about me. Besides I want to keep our marriage a secret until he returns. They would make me leave school and go home. It would disappoint Mama and Papa so bad." She wiped tears from her eyes. "I'm scared. I'm hoping Sam will be home soon. I need him here with me. He said he would come back for me by winter. That's just a few weeks away."

Rosa lifted one of Katherine's hands and patted it. "Miss Katherine, let's start takin' care of you and the chile you're carrin'. Ya make sure you eatin' right and drinkin' plenty of milk. I'll start fixin' food that will be good for you and the chile."

"Thank you. I just can't tell anyone else right now. You know how they would treat me if they knew."

"Don't matter what folks says or thinks. You's married and been blessed with a chile. I knows the Lawd's gonna look after ya. Besides, Sam's gonna come home to take care of ya b'fo long. It'll be 'tween me and you until ya wants them to know."

"I knew you would understand, Rosa."

At the end of each passing day, Katherine reached for her diary to write. Her words painted hours and days filled with hope, plans, and passion that she held for Sam.

Finally, one day in early November, while working in the kitchen with Rosa, Katherine was summoned to the front porch. The Abingdon Western Union clerk had a telegram for her. With no idea of what a telegram being sent to her would mean, her fingers trembled as she opened it. The other girls looked on excitedly. It read:

To Katherine Broadwater: From Sam:

Katherine, have not been able to think of nothing but you since leaving in August. I am in Appomattox. Fell off a wagon and busted my arm up. They are sending me home. Will be there by Friday. Send for your Ma and Pa and find you a pretty dress. We are going to have us a wedding party. Can't wait to see you. Love, Sam.

Katherine jumped and screamed. "Sam is coming home!" She held the telegram to her bosom. "We're going to have us a wedding party this weekend!"

Rosa stepped out to the porch to see what all the fuss was about. All the girls surrounded Katherine and she read the telegram out loud to them. When she looked up, Rosa was smiling and she gave Katherine a wink.

Over the next few days, they all began making plans for her wedding and party, still not knowing that she and Sam were already married.

Overwhelmed with joy, Katherine was also relieved because she was at the point of showing her pregnancy. She would have few people to turn to for help in a small town like Abingdon. Her life had changed, her secret burden lifted, and all she could think about was her life as Sam's wife.

In her diary she wrote:

Sam is coming home. My prayers are answered. I can't wait to be in his arms again. I can't wait to tell him about his child I am carrying. In three days, I can begin spending the rest of my life with him. I love you, Sam, and I will love you more and more tomorrow. I promise.

Three days seemed like an eternity to Katherine. Excited and cheerful, she made every effort to make herself even more beautiful. She couldn't wait to get her work done each day so she could prepare for her wedding party. She tried hard to make sure all the other girls would have a part, since they'd all asked to help.

Finally, Friday came. Rosa and Katherine finished fixing breakfast for everyone, and they sat down to eat.

"Once Sam gets home, reckon we will move to Galax. He said his pa has some land we can build our house on."

"We's gonna miss you, chile. No one else can light up this place like ya do."

"I'm sure other girls will come and take my place. They might find a boy and fall in love, too."

"Lawdy mercy! Let's hope not. Been too much of that goin' on round here this year." Rosa laughed, shaking her head.

"Mama and Papa should be here tomorrow. I don't know what Mama will do when I tell her I'm already married and going to have a baby."

"She'll be surprised sho' nuff," Rosa chuckled. "But yo mama knows what it's like to be young and lovin' someone. She's gonna hug ya and ask ya if you's happy. Once she knows her little girl's happy, nothin' else won't matter."

"The war's been hard on them with Papa not being able to find extra work. He's scared to leave the farm with all the Bluecoats swarming around. Mama wanted to get Rebecca, my sister next to me, to the boarding school. But because of the war, she won't be able to now."

"I hope the war will soon be over," Rosa agreed. "Lots of pretty girls needin' husbands 'round here. But a lot of de boys are leavin' to fight in the war and gettin' killed off."

"I know. I feel lucky Sam's coming back to me. Hope we can forget about the war and start a life somewhere away from the fighting."

"Yes, ya been blessed. Ya been blessed. Why don'tcha go and make yoself pretty for Sam? He's gonna be home b'fo you knows it. I got plenty of hep today."

Katherine stepped out on the back porch and found Judge Grey and a couple of men, whom she didn't know, talking in the yard. She went down and spoke, "Good morning, Judge Grey."

"Morning, Katherine. Can I help you?"

"Yes, I got a telegram from Sam saying he would be home today. He was in Appomattox. Would you know what time he might get here?"

"He probably rode down with the supply wagons to Damascus." Squinting up at the sun, Judge Grey shook his head thoughtfully. "He should be there early today if the Union doesn't hold them up somewhere. If he follows the footpath to Abingdon, then that's about a three-hour trip. He should make it here before sundown." He smiled and winked.

"Then, I'll watch for him. Thank you, Judge."

By late afternoon, Katherine was anxiously waiting for Sam. She stood outside on the back porch or paced back and forth in the back yard as the evening began to chill from a cold front moving in. Wearing her auburn-colored sweater and dressed in a long pale-blue dress, she continued to pace back and forth until rain began to fall and a thickening fog rushed nighttime into Abingdon.

She then went to the porch and sat until the air temperature dropped so much she could no longer stand to be outside. Rosa tried to comfort her. Thomas hung a couple of lanterns on the back porch, hoping Sam might see them and make his way to the house.

Finally, darkness, rain and bitter cold settled on Abingdon. Rosa urged Katherine to go rest, saying that Thomas would stay up and watch for Sam.

Katherine refused. Seated by the kitchen fireplace, her hands clasped in her lap, she knew Sam was trying to get home to her.

CHAPTER 14
Questions

Spencer's notes were filled with Katherine's story. Her passion brought the story to life. Spencer only hoped that his writing would do it justice once he completed his book. As he attentively wrote every detail she spoke, he felt he was only moments away from knowing what happened between Katherine and Sam.

Katherine wiped a tear from her cheek.

Spencer reached over and laid a hand on hers. "Take your time, Katherine. We can take a break if you need one."

Spencer's cell phone began to ring. Somewhat agitated, he reached for it, "Hello, Spencer here."

"Hello, Spencer, this is Bernice. I came by the Inn hoping I would catch you. I've been over at the historical society today. I did some research on this girl named Katherine Broadwater you wanted me to check on for you. I've found some interesting information I want to share with you."

Not wanting to say anything to let Katherine know he was talking about her, Spencer replied, "That's good. I'll meet you in the lobby in just a minute." Then he thought. *If I leave, she might walk away again.*

He turned back to the phone.

"Bernice, would you mind meeting me at the back entrance instead? I'll stand on the steps and wait for you. I'll tell you why once you get here."

"I'm on my way. Let me tell you what I've found. First, I checked all phone directories in the counties surrounding Abingdon to see if there was any Broadwater listed. I didn't find any. I then went to the historical society, as you requested, and searched through the archives to see if they had names of the girls who attended the boarding school back in the nineteenth century. They did, and there was a girl named Katherine Broadwater who attended the school there from 1862 to 1865. That was the same time the school was used as a hospital during the Civil War."

Spencer became excited hearing the information. "Bernice, there is someone here with me you have to meet. I'll meet you at the top of the steps. See you in a minute." He flipped his phone off and turned his attention back to Katherine. "I've got someone coming out to meet me on the steps." He pointed to the back of the Inn. "I'm going to stand up there and wait for her. I want you to meet her when she gets here. She's on her way now."

Katherine only stared and remained where he left her.

Spencer walked up the steps where he would have full view, so she wouldn't be able to leave without him seeing her go. With the information Bernice had given him, he realized that Katherine or whoever this girl was, was actually telling him about a Katherine Broadwater who attended this boarding school during the Civil War. Was she a relative or just someone who had been able to read about the girl's life somewhere? The more Spencer thought about her, the more questions he had. At last, he was going to get answers to his questions.

The door opened and Spencer glanced around to find Bernice. "Thanks for coming out to meet me. I would like for you to meet Katherine Broadwater." He pointed and looked back toward Katherine...but he saw no one. Speechless, knowing that there was no way Katherine could've walked away in the few seconds he turned his head, he walked down the steps to the center of the patio. He turned in circles a couple of times looking everywhere and finally said, "She's gone."

"Who's gone?" Bernice asked, inspecting Spencer closely.

"Katherine was sitting here with me and just vanished." He pointed at the chair where she'd been sitting.

"Maybe she walked away," Bernice said, walking down the steps.

"No, you don't understand." Spencer began to pace back and forth. "I wanted you to come out and meet me here so she wouldn't leave. I was watching her from the steps while waiting for you and turned my head for only a second. She didn't walk away, she vanished."

"People don't just up and disappear, Spencer."

"I knew something wasn't normal about her." He shook his head, agitated. "Her accent, the old-fashioned clothes she wore and how she only talked about her life in the nineteenth century. I suspected that she might be..." Spencer hesitated when he saw Bernice staring at him quizzically.

"She might be what?" Bernice asked, tilting her head sideways and frowning.

"Bernice, I know none of this looks good or makes sense to you. But...but I think this Katherine that I've been talking to is from the past or something." He put his hands in his pockets and stared down at his feet. "I know she's not from around here or at least not from this time." He looked up, and then said quietly, "I think she's a ghost."

"A ghost! Spencer, are you feeling well?" Bernice asked as she peered at him.

Spencer shook his head, took a deep breath and threw up his hands, trying to find the words to convince Bernice that Katherine existed or at least her ghost did.

The pool waitress walked from the back door and down to them. She had walked past them earlier, so Spencer thought that maybe she had seen Katherine. He stopped her as she walked by.

"When you walked by today did you happen to look over and see the young lady who was sitting with me at this table?"

"No, I'm sorry. I didn't see anyone." She shook her head.

"You must have." Spencer spoke firmly. "We sat out here and talked for two hours. She was a very young, pretty girl, and there's no way you couldn't have seen her."

"Mr. Aubreys, I never noticed either of you at the table. I've only been out here a couple of times today. I never looked over that way. If I had known you were there, then I would've offered beverages to you. I'm sorry I missed you." She shrugged her shoulders.

"No, I'm sorry. I'm sorry for putting you on the spot."

As the waitress turned to walk away, she glanced at Bernice, rolled her eyes up and nodded toward Spencer.

"Spencer, are you sure you're feeling okay?" Bernice asked again. "Is there something I can do to help, or maybe call someone for you?"

"No, Bernice, I'm fine. Just give me a minute to get my thoughts together. I don't know what Katherine is or what her purpose for telling me this story was. But it's obvious she's from the past. Whether she's a ghost, spirit, or just some lost soul, I don't know what you'd call her."

He put his face in his hands and tried to think of how to convince Bernice that he wasn't flipping out, and then remembered. "I know how to prove to you that Katherine does exist. There was a young couple here earlier and their names were…oh yes, Todd and Judi. They were looking at the gazebo for their wedding sometime next year. They talked to Katherine and me on the sidewalk this morning. Maybe someone here knows them."

"I'll speak to Julia before I leave and find out who they were." She wrote their names down.

"Also, if Katherine were listed at the historical society as a student, could you find out who her mom and dad were? She said her mother's name was Clara and her dad's name was Zack, named after his dad whose name was Zackary. She was born in 1849 and had a sister named Rebecca." He looked at her expression of disbelief, and then shrugged, his hands out. "How would I know all of this if she didn't tell me?"

"You do have a lot of facts about her." Bernice thought for a second. "Yes, I guess I could try to do some research. Maybe it will tell us something."

"Also…" Spencer raised his finger and asked, "Can you trace her family to present-day Abingdon? Is it possible to find some relative in her family we could talk to? Maybe they would know something about Katherine."

"I suppose I could find something in the genealogy records that might lead me to a relative. I'll try. In the meantime, are you sure I can't help with anything else?"

"No, Bernice, just please call if you find out anything." He walked over to the table to get his laptop.

Bernice walked away and looked back, frowning before entering the Inn.

In the hallway near the front lobby, Bernice saw the waitress who was outside with them. She stopped her and asked, "I couldn't help but overhear your conversation with Mr. Aubreys. I'm doing some research work for him at the request of a friend. What have you noticed about him? Is he acting okay?"

"We really aren't allowed to talk about our guests." Looking around nervously, she leaned forward and whispered. "A couple of other girls and I have noticed that he sits and writes for hours. He's ordered beverages a couple of times for two people and when we take them to him, he always talks about some girl named Katherine that had supposedly just walked off. We just go along with it, even though it seems a little strange."

"How about this girl he keeps talking about named Katherine?"

"He's asked everyone at the Inn about her." She shrugged her shoulders. "But no one has seen her or knows who she is."

"Thank you for the information." Bernice walked away, shaking her head, and stopped by the front desk, then motioned Julia over. "Can I get some information from you?"

"Sure, Bernice, how can I help you?"

"Is there a young couple here, a Todd and Judi? I don't know their last names. I need to ask them something."

Glancing around, Julia said, "I know who you're talking about, but they aren't here. They were looking at the gazebo to possibly have their wedding here next June. They were only passing through and haven't made any plans with us yet."

Bernice sighed. "Well, at least I wanted to give him the benefit of the doubt." Leaning forward, she whispered, "It's Spencer. He said he's been talking to a ghost."

"Oh, my!" Julia's eyes widened. "Why would he say that?"

"That's what I intend to find out. I guess it's time I called Elaine and tell her what's going on."

Leaving the Inn, Bernice called her as soon as she got down the steps.

"Hello, Bernice," Elaine answered. "I'm glad you called. I've been wondering how the work with Spencer is going."

"I'm not sure. Regretfully, we may have a problem. I just came by the Inn to give Spencer some information about a Katherine Broadwater we spoke about earlier. I couldn't find anyone in or near Abingdon with that name. But I did find the name registered as one of the students who attended school here when the Inn was a girl's boarding school in the nineteenth century. She was registered when the school was used as a hospital during the Civil War." Bernice stopped walking and stood beside her car.

"Is that a problem?" Elaine asked.

"Well, maybe not. I came by the Inn to see Spencer to tell him what I had found out about this girl named Broadwater he had me checking on. He asked me to meet him out back at the steps and wanted me to meet someone. I walked out, and he started to introduce me to a Katherine Broadwater he claimed he had been talking to, but there was no one there. He acted surprised and somewhat shaken up."

"I don't understand, Bernice. Did she leave or something?"

"No, here's the weird part." She put her hand on her hip and looked around. "He said that Katherine was a ghost or spirit or something."

"Oh, my! That sounds so out of character for him. What do you think made him say that?"

"I don't know. I spoke to one of the waitresses and she said when he orders beverages, he always orders for two. But when she delivers them to him, he's always alone and makes excuses about this Katherine disappearing or something."

"So no one else has seen this girl he's talking about?"

"That's right. He acted nervous, plus it looks like he hasn't shaved since he's been here. I offered him help, but he said everything was fine. He's just so adamant and obsessed with this Katherine. Where do you think this is coming from?" She leaned against her car as she placed the phone between her shoulder and ear, digging in her purse for her keys.

"I'm not sure, Bernice. I know he's a great writer and had a large following for his work in the newspaper. He and his wife have been separated for four months, and I know that has bothered him a lot."

Bernice rolled her eyes and pulled her keys from her purse. "Do you think it's substance abuse?"

"No, I know Spencer too well. He'd never do that."

"He's also asked me to continue to find out what I can about this Katherine Broadwater who attended the boarding school. He even gave me what he said was her mother and father's names, the date she was born and a sister's name. He said Katherine told him all of this." Opening the car door, she threw her purse in.

"Will you be able to do that since she was born in the nineteenth century?"

"Yes." She slid into the car seat. "I'll search the archives and some of the genealogy records. I can probably trace someone in the family up to the present if they still live in this area."

"Why don't you try that? In the meantime, I'll plan to drive down tomorrow evening instead of waiting till Saturday. I need to talk with him and see what's going on."

"I'd feel better if you were here." Bernice breathed a sigh of relief. "Especially if I need to sit and speak with him again."

"I'll also call Miriam without letting her in on what's going on. Maybe she can tell me something that'll give us a clue. If he's not harassing anyone or breaking the law, though, there's not much we can do anyway."

"I didn't know what else to do," she said, fitting her keys into the ignition. "Since you're footing the bill, I thought the least I could do was let you in on what's happening."

"You did the right thing. You work on finding out more about Katherine, and I'll try to find out more from Miriam."

"Then I'll see you tomorrow evening?"

"Yes. Maybe we can have dinner at the Inn."

"I look forward to it. See you then." She cranked her car and drove away.

CHAPTER 15
Another Stormy Night

In the warmth of the fire logs in his room, Spencer sat at the table and worked on Katherine's story. The comfort of the fire-lit room against another cold, stormy night inspired him to write for hours, and he lost track of time. Finally, hearing his stomach growl, he realized it was nine-thirty, and he decided to go down to the dining room to eat before they closed at ten o'clock.

On his way out the door, his cell phone rang. It was Miriam. "Hello, Miriam," he answered.

"Hello, Spencer. I wanted to call and check to see how your project is going. Did I call at a bad time?"

Surprised that she'd called, he sat down in a wingback chair in front of the fireplace. "No, I'm actually taking a break. I've been sitting here writing for hours, and time got away from me."

"What've you decided to write about?"

Not wanting to tell Miriam anymore than he had to about his encounter with Katherine, he decided to keep the information brief. "I'm trying to write a story about a young boy and girl's life together during the Civil War."

"How did you come up with that idea?"

"This inn that I'm staying in is full of history. It was once a boarding school for girls in the nineteenth century and used as a hospital for soldiers during the Civil War. I'm trying to put a story together around what someone mentioned to me."

"How are you feeling?" she asked.

"I feel fine. Just a little tired. I haven't been able to sleep well since coming here." He rubbed his eyes. "You'd think with the rainy nights and a warm fire that I would go out like a light. I've got a lot on my mind, I guess."

"Elaine called earlier. She didn't come out and say it but, from her conversation, I could tell she was a little concerned about you."

Spencer leaned forward and placed his elbows on his legs to rest his forehead in a hand, thinking, *Now I know the real reason she called.* "I guess that must be coming from her friend, Bernice Ferguson. She's a historian who's been doing some research for me. She came by today to give me information and while she was here, I wanted her to meet someone. However, the person I wanted her to meet left suddenly and it didn't turn out the way I planned. So she must've called Elaine."

"I know how stressed out you get when you have a lot on your mind. Dealing with your job loss, our separation, and all the effort you always put into your writing I'm sure is wearing you down."

"Yes, but I'll figure it out eventually. Maybe once I get home I'll start looking for work again. I'd like to stay in Charlottesville, but if I have to move, I will." He sat up in the chair and reached for his squeeze ball.

"Spencer, you're not the only one hurting from our breakup, you know."

"I know, Miriam, but the kids will adjust. They've got family and careers of their own started now." Leaning back, he squeezed the ball.

"I'm not talking about the kids." She raised her voice. "I'm talking about me. Can't you understand? We've known each other for almost thirty years and were married for twenty-seven of those years. Did you think you could just walk out of my life and I would move on like you were never a part of it? Is that the way you are dealing with it?" The agitation in her voice was clear.

"No, Miriam, I'm sorry. I thought you meant the kids." He stood and began to pace the room, squeezing his stress ball.

"You just don't get it, do you? You were my first love and probably my last," she said angrily. "I'll admit that our breakup was both our faults. We should've never let it come to this. But we both screwed up and forgot what our priorities were."

"I agree, Miriam. We did screw up. I just don't know what to do about it!" He shouted, "What do you want me to do about it?" He threw the stress ball across the room, bouncing it off the wall, knocking the glass with the flower to the floor.

"I don't have answers for us, Spencer!" She raised her voice even louder. "I wish I did. It's obvious you stay stressed out and on edge about something all the time. I can't call and have a conversation without your getting upset with me." She began to cry.

"I'm not upset because you called," he said more softly, as he sat down on the sofa. "I'm like you, just trying to figure us out."

"I was hoping that once we separated, we'd both realize that what we had was important." Clearing her throat, she choked back a sob. "But now I feel that every time I talk to you, we grow more and more apart. I just can't deal with this anymore."

Spencer took a deep breath and lowered his head, "I didn't mean to upset you, Miriam."

"You didn't, I did it to myself," she snapped. "I had no business calling you tonight. I called out of concern because Elaine called. I won't make this mistake again, and you won't have to worry about me bothering you anymore. I promise."

Spencer lay back on the sofa. In a lowered voice, he said, "When I get home we'll get together and figure out what we need to do, Miriam. I know what this is doing to you...and me. We need to make a decision and get on with our lives."

There was a pause...then Miriam said quietly, "Goodbye, Spencer." The phone clicked.

Spencer sat up, placed his face in his hands and thought. *How much more can one man take? No job, headed toward divorce, and now some ghost or something from the past is talking to me. Am I imagining this, or am I going crazy? Why has Katherine contacted me, and what am I to do with her story? What should I do about Miriam and me? I've just got to find a way to work through this.*

His stomach in a knot, Spencer stood and checked his wrist watch. It was after ten o'clock. *I've missed dinner, and there's no way I'm going out in this rain. I'll just go to the bar. Maybe they'll have something I can snack on.*

As he stood to leave, the flower that Katherine picked caught his attention. Retrieving it from the floor, and noticing it had wilted, he tossed it in the trash.

The bar was empty except for a young barmaid cleaning up and putting things in order. She was a tall woman in her mid-twenties with long, brown hair that complemented the uniform she wore.

"Good evening, sir. Can I get you a drink?" she asked with a gracious smile.

"Yes, how about a gin and tonic and maybe a bowl of that snack mix?"

"Sure." She poured the snack mix into a bowl and passed it to him.

Reaching for a bottle of gin, she asked, "Are you staying here at the Inn?"

"Yes."

"For business or pleasure?"

"I'm trying to do some writing and hope to get an outline of a book finished."

Setting the drink on the bar, she asked, "What kind of book?"

"Hopefully one that will sell." He laughed and sipped his drink. "This is my second one. Wrote one a few years back and made a few bucks on it. I have an agent who's become a close friend. She sent me down to do some research, hoping that I would find something interesting to inspire me." He reached for a handful of snack mix.

"Having any luck?"

"Actually, I have. I met this young girl who has been telling me about a romance that took place between a young boy and girl in the nineteenth century. It happened when the Inn was used as a hospital during the Civil War." He sipped his drink while watching her arrange glasses on a rack.

"That sounds interesting." She glanced at him. "Who is she?"

"She said her name is Katherine Broadwater. She kind of just drops in and out of here to tell me this story that happened almost a century and half ago. No one at the Inn seems to know anything about her and claim they've never seen her. I think she's a ghost, but other people are beginning to think I'm crazy." He gauged her reaction.

"Maybe she is a ghost. Can I get you another drink? You downed that one pretty fast."

"No, one's my limit. But I will have a glass of water. I was so busy writing I forgot to come down for dinner."

"It's too late to order from the bar menu." She glanced back at the wall clock. "But I can call the kitchen and see if they could fix you a cold plate or something." She set the glass of water on the bar.

"No, I'm fine." He shook his head and sighed. "Don't want to eat a lot now because I'm going up to bed in a minute. Back to what you said earlier, though. Do you believe in ghosts?" He reached for the glass.

"Yes, I do. At least, I think it's one of those sixth sense things that people have. Some of us have it, and some don't. I know people who have seen things they can't explain." She folded her arms and leaned on the bar.

"Do you think there are ghosts at this inn?"

"I would think so. There are actually documented stories about some of the encounters other guests have had. There's a book about the ghost at this inn, the theater, and a lot of houses in Abingdon. A lot of the sightings seem to be from the Civil War era."

"What are some of the ghost stories about the Inn?" He shook his glass, clinking the ice cubes.

"Guests have heard violin music playing, doors flying open, feeling a chill in their room." She shivered as she described the anomalies. "Some even claim they've seen young girls walking the hallways, searching for their lost lovers. We actually have a lady who comes in twice a week and does ghost tours for our visitors."

"Yes, I met her Tuesday when I arrived." He smiled and nodded.

"You ready for more snack mix?" she asked, reaching for his bowl.

"No, thank you. I should survive till breakfast." He stood up and laid seven dollars on the counter.

"Here's your tab. By the way, what's your name? I may want a copy of your book when it comes out." She grabbed a pen and pad.

"Thanks for the vote of confidence. Spencer Aubreys is the name. Thanks for chatting with me. I enjoyed the company."

"Thank you. I hope you won't have any encounters with the spirits on the way to your room." She looked up from the writing pad and grinned.

"As long as they're friendly, I won't mind. Good night." He smiled and turned away.

Since the halls were quiet and no one was stirring, he decided to walk through the Inn before returning to his room. On the second floor was a hall breezeway that connected another wing to the Inn. Walking through the breezeway, he stopped, leaned against a window post, and gazed out into the darkness. Thoughts of Miriam and their earlier conversation were heavy on his mind as he stood listening to the falling rain blowing against the large windowpanes. *Maybe I haven't been fair to Miriam, thinking that somehow, or some way, I could fix our marriage. She and I are both hurting and maybe closure is what we both need to get this behind us so we can get on with our lives. After all, maybe I've been selfish, wanting her back and longing for things to be the way they once were. Aren't her wants and needs important also? We can't even have a phone conversation anymore without getting upset with each other. If I have nothing more to give her, I should set her free. At least, maybe she will eventually find happiness. When I get home, hopefully we can be civil about it and finalize our separation. I guess when it's over, it's over.* Spencer felt tears brimming in his eyes.

The sound of music caught his attention; it was a violin playing. It sounded so close by that Spencer listened to hear from what direction it was coming. The clear, smooth melody sounded like a familiar sad song. Looking around for the speaker system that carried the music, Spencer turned the corner and met Allen, the bellhop.

"Evening, Mr. Aubreys. I see that you are still up."

"Yes, I was just taking a stroll before going up to bed. I've been listening to violin music playing. It sounded live. I was looking for the speaker system to see where the music was coming from." He glanced around.

Allen turned his head in a couple of directions and listened, but the music had ceased. "We don't have a speaker system, and we don't play music in the hallways." He raised his eyebrows questioningly.

Spencer paced down the hallway and back, listening. "There was definitely music playing. I stood here and listened to it for several minutes."

"Then it must've come from one of the guest rooms." Allen pointed down the hall. "Maybe someone had their TV on."

"Maybe so." Spencer threw up his hands and turned away. "I'm going up to get some rest. Good night, Allen."

"Good night, Mr. Aubreys."

In his room, Spencer thought about the music in the hallway and where it could possibly have come from. *It couldn't be coming from a guest's room because it was too clear and loud. And what about the barmaid's comment that violin music playing was one of the haunt-*

ings of the Inn? Am I now hearing things, and what does that mean? Was this Elizabeth playing her violin for me?

While sitting at the table and reviewing his writing for the day, he realized that he wouldn't be able to finish the story unless Katherine returned. And what would he do if she appeared again, since it was becoming obvious to him she was a ghost? What was her *purpose* for contacting me? After reviewing his notes, he turned the fireplace gas off and headed to bed.

He removed his clothing and slipped under the cover. Listening to the rain fall outside and staring into the darkness, he hoped that sleep would soon come to his exhausted body and mind. Thinking about Miriam, and then about Katherine, he tossed and turned through another stormy night.

CHAPTER 16
Looking for Katherine

Laughter from outside woke Spencer. Opening his eyes and looking toward the window, he saw that daylight had come. It had been 2:30 a.m. when he last checked the time. Tired and emotionally exhausted, with both Miriam and Katherine in his thoughts, his body would not yield to sleep.

Thinking of the unfinished story, his mind first turned to Katherine. *I have to find her so I can learn what happened between her and Sam. I would hate to get this far with her story and just make up something. I need to find Katherine and let her tell me the end. What should I do if I see her again, now that I believe she's a ghost? I guess I can figure that out if I see her.*

Stepping from the shower and reaching for the towel to dry off, he turned to the wash basin and glanced into the mirror. He saw his now four-day-old beard. *No wonder everyone is beginning to have doubts about me. I need to get a razor and shave.* He had often heard Miriam say, "I don't know how you ever made it on your own. You could never make it without me now." *Regretfully, I'm beginning to agree with her.*

Dressed in a pair of jeans and a brown, suede shirt, he grabbed a jacket on the way out and walked down to the front porch to see how cold it was

"Morning, Mr. Aubreys," Allen greeted him.

"Good morning, Allen." Spencer wondered when the man ever rested. He walked to the porch rail and looked out. "Do we see sunshine today or more fog and rain?"

"More of the same," Allen replied. "But we're supposed to get icing tonight. Tomorrow, cold temperatures but with lots of sunshine."

Spencer turned toward him and nodded, "Whatever it takes to get the sun in here is fine by me."

"Can I get your car and bring it up for you?" Allen asked.

Shaking his head, Spencer replied, "No, I'm going down for breakfast and then maybe take another walk on the Creeper Trail. It's my last day here."

"Have a nice day, Mr. Aubreys."

After breakfast, Spencer walked around the back lot. Hoping that by chance Katherine would show up, he came to the bush that had flowers with pink petals and a yellow center. Picking a flower and sliding his finger over it, he couldn't help but think of Katherine and her fascination with these flowers.

After an hour of walking around the back lot, hoping to see Katherine again but having no luck, he turned toward the Creeper Trail. On the way there, he passed the bike shop. The elderly shopkeeper was lining up bikes in the bike rack out front.

Spencer greeted him with a cheerful, "Good morning."

"Good morning," the older gentlemen replied. "Oh, you're the fellow that got a bike from me late in the afternoon a couple of days back, aren't you?" He raised his hand to stop him.

"Yes, I did." Spencer stopped.

"Do you remember the torn, red-dyed ten dollar bill I gave you?"

"Yes, I remember."

"One of our bikers found it on the trail. Said he spoke to a biker standing at that exact spot the evening before. Figured you dropped it out of your pocket. He asked if he could leave it here in case you came by. I told him that I'd given it to you and would remember you if you came back."

"I gave it to a young boy. Said he was coming home from the war. Looked like he could use the money. He must've dropped it."

"Here, let me get it for you." The man turned and walked toward the shop. "It's not mine. You can do what you want with it."

As the older man stepped into the shop, Spencer waited and thought about Samuel. *He must've dropped the money, and he really looked like he could use it. Oh well, maybe I'll see him before I leave Abingdon.*

Returning, the shopkeeper gave the money to Spencer. "Here you go, sir. Do you want a bike?"

"No, I'm walking the trail today. I need to think some things through. The trail seems like a good place to do it. Thanks for returning the money."

"It was the other biker, not me. Have a good day." He returned to setting bikes in the bike rack.

Walking the trail, Spencer thought about the previous day's events—the story Katherine shared with him and Bernice's reaction to his telling her Katherine was a ghost. Trying to sort it out, he thought, *Am I going crazy and just imagining all of this?* Then, he thought about the many pages of writing he had. *No, something's going on here. I need to find Katherine and prove to everyone that she does exist.* He continued up the trail.

Autumn leaves, stripped by rain, blanketed the trail. A carpet of reddish-orange, yellow and brown covered his path, disappearing into the mist of fog ahead of him, as if leading him to oblivion.

Finally, he came to a wooden fence where two horses stood attentively, as though waiting for someone. Spencer moved closer and raised a hand to rub one of them on the neck. He remembered the times he and Miriam used to do a lot of horseback riding when they were younger. The fun, laughter, and just being by each other's side was enough. What caused them to drift apart? And, more importantly, why did they let it happen? Longing to know if they could work things out if given the chance, he conceded they'd let it go too far to turn back now.

His cell phone rang. It was Bernice, and he became excited, wondering if she had more information about Katherine.

"Good morning, Bernice." He stood still to assure getting a good cell signal.

"Good morning, Spencer. I hope I haven't caught you at a bad time."

"No, not at all. I'm taking a walk on the Creeper Trail." He stepped back onto the path.

"Good for you. The reason I'm calling is I have more information on the Katherine Broadwater who lived in the nineteenth century."

"Great! What've you found out?" Spencer stood motionless, not wanting to miss anything Bernice said.

"I tried doing a genealogy search on Katherine Broadwater, thinking if she got married, there would have been a name change. I was wrong. She did get married, but her name never changed. She had a child, a girl named Samantha Lynn. From Samantha, I traced relatives and located an elderly lady who is a descendant of Katherine's. Her name is Christine Katherine Hudson. She is one of her great-grandchildren."

"Then, she should know Katherine's life story and what happened to her and Sam. How can I get in touch with her?" Spencer began walking back toward Abingdon.

"I've already called Christine and explained that you are a writer and would possibly like to speak with her. She's agreed to meet you and said something about an old diary that her great-grandmother kept. It's been passed down to the oldest daughter over the last three generations."

"That's great." *It must be the diary Katherine told me about.* Spencer walked faster. "Can you give me her phone number? I'd like to meet with her today if possible."

"I'll call and see what I can arrange. Also..." she paused again.

"Bernice, are you still there?" Spencer looked at his phone to see if he still had a signal.

"Yes, I wanted to tell you that Katherine was born in 1849 and that her mother and father's names were Clara and Zack.

131

Her father's dad was named Zackary, and she did have a sister named Rebecca."

"Thanks, Bernice," he said quickly. His thoughts racing ahead, he closed his phone without even saying goodbye.

Excited, Spencer walked even faster toward Abingdon. A few minutes later, he began running, anxiously anticipating what more he might find out. *At least it might validate my meetings with Katherine and the story she told me.*

Finally making it back to the Inn, he ran onto the front porch and into the lobby. Julia glanced up from the counter and asked, "Mr. Aubreys, are you okay?"

"Yes, I'm fine," he answered, pausing to catch his breath. "Bernice called while I was on the trail and had some information I needed. May I borrow a pen and paper, please?"

"Sure." She handed them to him.

He called Bernice and learned that Christine Hudson could meet him immediately. She gave him directions.

Looking at his watch, he saw that it was twelve o'clock and it would take him about thirty minutes to drive to Lebanon where Christine lived. He ran to his car but dropped his keys before he could get his door open. Then he forced himself to slow down and control his excitement. Finally, he could find out more about Katherine but it wouldn't matter if it took a few minutes longer if he got there safely. Breathing evenly, he opened his door and got in, wondering why in the world Katherine had chosen to tell her story to him and no one else at the Inn. *Why has she connected with me and no one else at the Inn?*

CHAPTER 17
The Diary

Once on the road to Lebanon, Spencer wondered if he should say anything to Christine about her great-grandmother visiting him three times at the Inn. *Maybe I'll just wait and see if I think she can handle the information once I meet her.*

Spencer saw a mailbox with the name and numbers he was looking for. Turning onto a narrow, graveled drive that wound and climbed for several hundred feet, he came to a white country house with wooden rockers on the large front porch. Parking beside a pickup truck, he walked to the front door and knocked. A tall, young girl with short hair, dressed in jeans and a white pullover came to the door.

"Hi, my name is Spencer Aubreys. Bernice Ferguson called earlier, and I'm to meet Christine."

"Yes, she's expecting you. My name is Kathy. Christine is my grandmother. Please come in."

Following the young girl into the house, Spencer couldn't help but notice the resemblance between her and Katherine. She had the same auburn-colored hair, blue eyes and narrow cheekbones but was much taller. Although she didn't speak with the same southern accent, she could easily pass as Katherine's sister.

Once in the living room, Spencer saw a small, gray-haired lady, wearing glasses, sitting in a rocker by the window, knitting.

"Grandma, Mr. Aubreys is here to see you." Kathy glanced toward him, smiling.

The woman put down her needlework and started to get up, but Spencer stopped her.

"Please, keep your seat. I'll just sit here in this other chair by the window if that's okay."

"Please do, Mr. Aubreys." She removed her glasses as she spoke.

"Just call me Spencer, and please, don't let me stop you from knitting." He pointed to the yarn she'd laid aside.

"Quite all right, Mr. Aubreys, or Spencer. My eyes are getting tired and need a rest." She looked at her hands. "My hands are beginning to shake so bad, I'm not going to be able to knit much longer anyway."

"I really appreciate your seeing me on short notice." He folded his hands on his lap.

"Bernice said you're trying to find out about someone in our family. She said you were a writer and needed information to finish a story."

"That's correct. I'm actually trying to put together a story someone is telling me. She said her name is Katherine." Spencer hesitated, watching her closely, feeling that it was best not to tell her that her great-grandmother had possibly visited him. "The story she told me took place in Abingdon during the Civil War."

"Grandma," Kathy said as she re-entered the room. "I need to run a couple of errands and pick David up from work. Is there anything I can get for you while I'm out?"

"I have a list on the kitchen counter with money. Can you stop and get some groceries for me after picking up David?"

"I'll be glad to." She turned to Spencer with another smile and said, "It's nice meeting you. Is there anything I can get for you before I leave, maybe a beverage?"

"No, thanks, I'm fine. It's good to meet you, too, Kathy." Spencer continued to marvel over the resemblance she had to Katherine.

"Drive carefully, Kathy, and watch your speed," her grandmother reminded her.

"I will. I should be back shortly. Love ya, Grandma."

"Love you, too, dear." She watched Kathy leave, and then shifted her gaze to Spencer.

"Young people just don't have a chance anymore. She's been laid off from her job, and her husband David is working only thirty-two hours a week. They're already two payments behind on their mortgage. I'm afraid they're going to lose their home. I'm trying to help them, but I don't know if it'll be enough." She clasped her hands and stared down.

"I'm sorry to hear that. A lot of people are losing their jobs now. In fact, I lost mine two months ago."

"It's affecting all of us, isn't it? Kathy is my only granddaughter. Her parents were killed in an ice storm seven years ago. Her mother was my only child. They were in an automobile wreck here in the mountains. I finished raising her, and then she got married a couple of years ago. They were doing so well until recently." She sighed at length. "Oh, well, you didn't come here to listen to this."

"That's not a problem. I hope everything works out for them and you."

"Okay," Christine leaned toward Spencer. "This person you're talking to—her name is what?"

"She said her name is Katherine. She's been telling me about your great-grandmother."

Christine blinked her eyelids several times and said, "I don't know anyone who would know anything about my great-grandmother unless it's some distant relative of our family. My great-grandmother lived in the 1800s and was named Katherine Broadwater."

Spencer was relieved that she assumed Katherine was a stranger and not her actual great-grandmother. He knew that it would upset her if she thought Katherine was a visiting spirit.

"Bernice said you have a diary with some information about your great-grandmother Katherine."

"Yes, I do." She reached down into the bottom of her knitting basket and pulled out an object wrapped in clear plastic. "I got it

135

out when Bernice called. It's been a long time since I've looked at it."

She began to unwind the plastic from around it. Out of the wrap, it was also protected by an auburn-colored knitted cloth that she began to unwind, revealing the faded, white leather book.

"I apologize for the mothball smell. But I didn't want to lose this scarf. It's about to fall apart. My great-grandmother made it." She brushed the dust and lint from the diary.

"This is the diary that belonged to your great grandmother?" he asked, his curiosity whetted.

"Yes, it is. It has been passed down three generations to the oldest daughter in our family. We feel it's important to remember and keep the story of our great-grandmother alive. Since the pages were beginning to fall apart, I had them laminated years ago." She handed the diary to Spencer. "You're welcome to read from it if you want to. The pages are loose, so please be careful with them."

Spencer began turning the pages, reading, as Christine told him what she knew about her great-grandmother.

Spencer read, finding the words to be identical to Katherine's story. Unable to pull his eyes away once he started, he read while listening intently to Christine.

She came to the part where Katherine sat and waited for Sam. "Sam didn't show up that night, or the next day. The Union Army had attacked the supply wagons in the mountains near Damascus. Being outnumbered, the men scattered and ran off in different directions. Sam made it to the footpath where he could travel unnoticed on his way to Abingdon. It was late evening, raining, and the fog was heavy. That night a winter cold spell fell, and he found himself in wet freezing conditions without supplies or a lantern to travel by. Sometime during the night, the trail became dark and icy, causing him to slip and fall down an embankment, re-injuring his already shattered arm. With no light to guide him and losing his sense of direction, Sam covered himself with leaves and brush for protection from the cold, knowing he could not find his way out until morning. Two days later they found him frozen to death, clutching this knitted scarf. My great-grandmother made it for him. They said he was only a half-mile from Abingdon."

A lump arose in Spencer's throat as he read the page from Katherine's diary:

My heart grieves more than I can bear. They found Sam lying down a bank where he fell trying to come home to me. He was only a half-mile from reaching me, clutching the scarf I had made for him. The only reason I have to live and go on is because of the child I carry in my womb. All the love I have for Sam will now be given to our child. All of my time, my strength and courage will be to care for and raise our child so Sam would be proud of us. All of me, all my love, all my life will be to care for our child. Sam, I do it for you. I know I can't have you or be with you as long as I'm alive, but I hope and pray that someday when I pass on, we can be together again for eternity. Until then I will go on loving you every hour, every day for the rest of my life.

Spencer stared blankly at the page and rubbed tears from his eyes, apologizing to Christine. "I'm sorry for getting so emotional. But Katherine's life story is so touching, I couldn't help myself." Now he knew why Katherine was always standing outside. She was looking and waiting for Sam. Because of Katherine's visits with him, he knew how sincere her love for Sam was. He felt the tragic loss she endured.

"Quite all right, Spencer. I can assure you that everyone who has read this diary has shed tears over this wonderful and beautiful story Katherine left with us. She's been an inspiration to many of her descendants."

"What happened to her after Sam?"

"Being a young girl, pregnant and her ma and pa already having their hands full with six more kids, she stayed on and worked at the school as long as they let her. Sam's father and brother found out about Sam and came to Abingdon to take his body back to their home place. They met Katherine and learned that she was married to Sam and was having his baby. They wanted her to move back with them so they could help raise the child. But she refused and begged them to leave Sam in Abingdon so she would always be close to him.

"They did, but insisted on paying for her room and board so she would have a place of her own. In May of 1865, she had a baby girl named Samantha Katherine, who was my grandmother. She was named after both my great-grandmother and great-grandfather. Soon the war ended, and Katherine went back to school to finish her education while working with the local doctor to earn money. By then, seeing how determined she was to continue her education, all the townsfolk pitched in to help her."

Spencer asked, "Why didn't she ever remarry?"

"A lot of the young boys were killed during the war or never came back home after the war. Most men back then didn't want to marry a woman if she already had a child. Plus, she never mentioned in her diary about loving anyone else. While working with Doc Foster, she caught the fever after caring for someone they didn't know had it. Samantha was only a year and a half old. Katherine was quarantined and separated from Samantha. With no vaccine back then, she grew weaker and eventually died. Her last entry in the diary reflects that, if you would like to read it."

Spencer began to read: *My body grows weaker every hour, and I don't think I'm going to make it. Once my heart was broken because I lost Sam. Today my heart is breaking again for the child I'm going to leave behind. My child, Samantha, is so near but I can't hold her, love her, or even tell her goodbye. I can't wait to see Sam again and tell him about her. I know he'll be happy. My sister Rebecca, who has just gotten married, said she'll take care of her as if she were her child. I know Rebecca will. I don't know what I can tell Samantha to let her know what she's meant to me from the day she was born, except that every day of her life was a celebration of the love her papa, Sam, and I had for each other. As I go to join him in eternity, I want her to know that she will be in our hearts always. And if she ever needs help or her children or their children need help, then, if I'm able, I'll find some way to reach out and help. So, Samantha, remember every day of your life, you are beautiful.*

Someday when you read my diary and can know who your mama was, always remember that I'll love you forever, even in eternity.

Love,

Your Mama, Katherine

Spencer looked up at Christine and could see streaks of tears on her cheeks. She wiped at them and said, "Rebecca made sure that Samantha, my grandmother, knew all about her mother. She gave her this diary, and it has continued to be passed down to the oldest daughter in each generation. Also, our children carry the names of Sam and Katherine in every generation. We feel it's a way to honor them. Just as quick as the War Between the States brought them together, it also separated them. Even though they knew each other for only a few weeks, and their lives had tragic endings, their love for each other was real and a wonderful story worth keeping alive. Our great-grandmother was a beautiful young lady and an inspiration to all who have read about her. We want to keep her life, her love and her passion alive."

Spencer took a deep breath to compose himself.

Christine continued, "I had given this diary to my daughter, Kathy's mother. When she died, I got it back and had let Kathy read it. Today I'm going to give it to them as their keepsake. I'm hoping they will read it again and find some strength and hope through Katherine's words, especially now that they've fallen on hard times."

"Christine, you've given me a lot of information." Spencer sat up straight. "This is the same story that the young girl Katherine told me. With your permission, I'd like to complete the book I am writing. Sam and Katherine are a part of it."

"Yes," she said with a nod, "that would be nice. I think they had a great love and a story worth telling."

"I'll make sure some of the credits come back to your family, of course."

She glanced down. "Just knowing that others know about Sam and Katherine is enough." She looked up and smiled.

Spencer glanced at his watch and saw that they had been talking for two hours. His conversation with Mrs. Hudson and reading the faded yellow pages in the diary had yielded more than he expected. Overwhelmed with the new information, he wanted to get back to the Inn and finish his writing.

While excusing himself, though, Kathy returned home with David.

"Hi, Grandma, sorry we're running late. David needed to stop for an errand. Also, I went by the hardware store and picked up a couple of fall rose bushes they had on clearance to put on Grandma Katherine and Sam's graves." She held them up.

Christine stood up and shook her head. "You shouldn't have gone and done that. I know how tight money is for you."

Kathy shrugged her shoulders. "They only cost a couple of dollars, and I know Mama and Papa always kept flowers on the graves when they were here."

"Are Katherine and Sam's gravesites nearby?" Spencer asked.

"Yes," David pointed and said, "just on top of the hill above the house here. It's pretty up there."

Christine added, "When Katherine died, she and Sam were buried in separate cemeteries. My mother had them moved back here to the family plot before she passed away. She thought it was important for them to be together."

"May I see the gravesites?" Spencer asked.

"Sure," Kathy responded. "David, grab your pick and shovel, we can plant the rose bushes while we're at it."

Christine picked up her knitting. "I'm going to bow out of the trip, if you don't mind. I've gotten too old to climb up and down these hills."

"I understand." Spencer turned toward her and said, "Thanks for opening your home and heart for me. I'll try to do Katherine's story justice and send you a copy of the book when it's finished."

"Thank you. I'm sure you will, and please call me if I can do any more to help you."

Spencer, Kathy and David walked to the top of the hill. Spencer was amazed at the vast, beautiful view. For miles, rolling hills, ridges and forests reached as far as the eye could see.

As David began digging a hole to plant a rose bush, Spencer read the grave markers. "Katherine Broadwater, born March 15, 1849, died November 21, 1866. Reading Sam's marker, he gasped at what he saw, "Samuel Foley, born April 20, 1847, died November 12, 1864."

Kathy, puzzled by Spencer's reaction asked, "Are you okay, Mr. Aubreys?"

He stepped back and took a deep breath. "I'm all right. I didn't realize that Katherine's husband's name was Samuel Foley. I thought his name was Sam. She never mentioned his last name or I mean I never put them together."

"Pardon me," Kathy said, confused. "Sam is short for Samuel, the name his dad gave him from the Bible. Grandma Katherine never changed her name since he died before returning home. It's all mentioned in the diary."

"Yes, you're right. I guess I just didn't read it."

Noticing the date of Sam's death, he asked, "What is today's date?"

Kathy replied, "November twelfth, the same day Sam died one hundred and forty-six years ago."

Spencer now realized that the young boy he met on the Creeper Trail a couple of days earlier, who looked out of place, was Sam. It was obvious. He was trying to get home to Katherine.

Suddenly feeling uneasy and anxious, Spencer decided to leave and see if he could clear the cobwebs out of his brain. He had learned so much in the past few hours that he needed to sort it all out. "If you don't mind, I need to get back to Abingdon."

"No, sir. You do what you need to do, Mr. Aubreys," David replied, leaning on his shovel.

"Then I'm on my way. I'll be back in touch with you, I promise." He hurriedly walked away.

David turned to Kathy, "What got into him? He acted like he saw a ghost or something."

"I'm not sure. It must've been something on Sam's grave marker that upset him. And wasn't it strange that he said Katherine never mentioned Sam's last name to him?"

"That was real strange."

Shaken, Spencer went to his car and got in. Rubbing his face with his hands, he thought about Katherine and Sam, wondering why they had connected with him. *Was it purely a coincidence that I was in the right place and time? What am I to do now that I know the ending to Katherine's life story? It's a beautiful story, but such a tragic ending. What am I to do with it?*

CHAPTER 18
The Rescue

Spencer rushed back to Abingdon, trying to keep his speed at no more than ten miles over the speed limit. Not only had he gotten the end of the story, he was also able to read from the diary of which she had often spoken.

He now knew that it was no coincidence that the girl he had been talking to was Katherine Broadwater, and the young boy he met on the Creeper Trail was Samuel Foley, the love of her life. *What are they—ghosts, spirits or just two wandering souls that haven't found peace because of their love and longing to be together? Why have I been chosen as a contact? And what could I possibly do for them? I can't even convince anyone that they exist. What should I do if I see Katherine again?*

All of these questions raced through his mind until he finally pulled into the parking lot of the Inn in Abingdon.

When he walked inside the lobby, Julia saw him and motioned him over to the counter. "Elaine Wampler called. She's coming here this evening and wants to meet with you, if possible, around seven. She and Bernice have dinner planned at our dining room and invited you to join them."

Spencer glanced at his watch and saw that it was almost five o'clock. That gave him plenty of time to shower and change clothes. *She's probably coming down early to see firsthand what's going on since I'm sure Bernice has kept her informed. Maybe I can get the young couple Katherine and I talked with to validate that Katherine does exist.*

"Julia, I'll let her know about dinner later. Did Todd and Judi by any chance come back?"

Julia leaned on the counter. "No, Mr. Aubreys. They were passing through and looked at the gazebo to possibly have their wedding here next June."

He dropped his hand on the counter and mumbled, "I guess my only chance to prove that Katherine does exist is gone."

"Pardon me?"

"Nothing, Julia. I was just hoping they were here and could help me verify that they saw and spoke to Katherine Broadwater—the girl I've had trouble convincing everyone that she exists." He walked away, leaving Julia speechless, knowing that she too doubted his claim of visiting with Katherine.

Spencer went to his room and sat at the table by the window. Looking at notes and thinking about what he'd learned earlier, he began to wonder how he could make Katherine and Sam's love story that ended in tragedy have a good ending. In the end, though, feeling let down, he knew the story had to end the way Christine Hudson had shared and the diary ended.

Suddenly, the floor planks in the hallway alerted him that someone was coming up the hall. His room door flew open, sending a chill into the room. Stepping across the room to look outside, Spencer saw nothing and then remembered. *This is what happened the first time I walked outside and found Katherine. She must be out there again.* He grabbed his jacket and dashed downstairs and through the back door of the Inn.

On the pool deck looking over the back lot, he saw the thickening fog rolling in as a light drizzle fell. Feeling apprehensive, he stopped in mid-stride. Was Katherine some sort of a wandering spirit? What could he possibly do to help her? Hesitantly, he walked down past the gazebo for a closer look through the fog. About to give up on finding her, something caught his eye. Stepping across the mulch, he saw Katherine. She had her back to him, looking downhill toward the Creeper Trail. He now knew that in the 1800s it was called "the footpath" and was what she was referring to in her story.

He hesitated, and then softly called her name, "Katherine… Katherine…It's me, Spencer."

She turned and stared at him.

He moved closer. "Katherine, I know about you and Sam. I know what happened. Remember you told me about Sam, the war and him coming home to you?"

"Sam is coming home to me tonight. He promised," she said in a quivering voice.

Cautiously, and unsure what he should do, Spencer reached and took her small cold hand. "I know, Katherine. He's trying to get home to you. Believe me, I know he is."

"I need Sam. I need him here with me," she said sorrowfully. "I have news to tell him."

Spencer knew she wanted to tell Sam about their baby. But he also knew what the outcome would be. Listening to Katherine's plea for Sam to come home, he became restless. *Maybe I should go and try to find Sam. After all, I've seen him once on the Creeper Trail.*

Finally, he knew he had to try. Spencer took her by the arms and gazed into her teary, blue eyes. "Katherine, stay right here! I know where Sam is. I've seen him. He's on the footpath trying to get home to you. I'll go find him and bring him home to you. Stay here, Katherine. Don't give up. Please don't give up. Wait for Sam and me to get back." He turned and ran toward the Creeper Trail, adrenaline pushing him on.

Trembling and running up the trail in the now-heavy fog, he could barely see twenty feet ahead. He wished he'd brought a flashlight. Finally, he came to the place where he had first seen Sam earlier. The rain began falling heavier, and the air temperature dropped by the minute.

Spencer called out, "Samuel! Samuel! Can you hear me? I've come to help you get home. Samuel, come to me if you hear me. Katherine is waiting for you." He paced back and forth while the fog got denser. He could now see only a few feet ahead. Soaked by the cold rain, but refusing to give up, he continued to call Sam's name.

Finally, he saw Sam, his arm in a sling and clutching the auburn-colored knitted scarf in his hand. Spencer moved toward him.

"Sam, I've come to help you get home." He reached out to touch Sam, not knowing if it were possible to actually make contact.

Sam didn't move, but said, "I've got to get home to Katherine. I know she's waiting for me."

Spencer held onto his arm. It felt cold and wet. "Yes, Sam. Katherine is home waiting for you. Come, let me help you."

Sam appeared weak and was shivering from the cold, so Spencer removed his coat and put it around his shoulders. Lifting Sam's free arm, he put it over his shoulders to lead him down the trail.

Daylight was fading fast, and Spencer figured they had only a short time before everything went dark and they wouldn't be able to see how to travel. A cold wind pushed them along, the rain falling heavier. He tried to lead Sam on, talking to him about Katherine, step by step trying to pick up their pace. Knowing the urgency to get off the trail before there was no light to travel by, he felt desperation grip him in the downpour of frigid rain.

Suddenly, Spencer stepped on slippery leaves on the muddy shoulder of a steep bank. It gave way as he lost his balance and fell. He tried to push Sam back but with no luck, and he, too, fell over the bank. They slid down the steep incline toward the creek. They both frantically clawed and grabbed at every bush or tree, Sam trying to break his fall with his good arm. Spencer grabbed Sam's wrist, then caught a sapling in his path, which broke their slide. Holding firmly onto Sam, Spencer lay still to catch his breath. Finally, looking down, he saw that they were only a few feet from falling off a cliff bank into a rocky creek full of rushing water. Looking back uphill, he saw they had at least twenty feet of climbing to do to get back on the trail. Firmly holding Sam, with all his might he pulled him back up the hill, inch by inch. Fully exhausted, they finally made it. Spencer thought about what was in the diary. *This must be what happened to Sam when he was trying to get home to Katherine and never made it. Maybe with me being here to help will change their story. I hope so.*

He helped Sam back to his feet, placed his coat back over his shoulders and braced him with an arm. "Come on, Sam. We don't have far to go." Fighting fatigue, bruised and feeling cold, he knew they had no choice but to walk on. He talked to Sam every step they took to give him hope. "Don't give up on making it. Katherine loves you and needs you. Stay with me, Sam. We're gonna make it."

After what seemed like hours, near the point of total fatigue, Spencer made it to the end of the trail holding onto Sam. He saw the lights of the Inn and continued up the hill. Every step was a challenge.

Practically carrying Sam and fighting to stay on his feet, he came to the spot where he had left Katherine. He held firmly to Sam, while calling out to her.

"Katherine, Katherine, we're here! I've brought Sam home to you!" He repeated it several times, hoping she would appear and greet them.

When he saw her, she was only a few feet away, gazing at them, yet not making a move. Sam slipped his arm off Spencer, mustering up strength to walk on his own. Taking one step at a time, never taking his eyes off Katherine, he finally reached her. Taking the knitted scarf that was in his hand, he draped it around her neck and smiled. He then stepped back, extended his arm and opened his palm to her. Crying but smiling, she placed her hand into his palm. He pulled her close, until their bodies molded together. Katherine cried on his shoulder while Samuel held her tightly in the heavy downpour, his face buried in her hair. Fog and darkness engulfed them. Spencer could only faintly see them together in the darkness, which deepened until he could no longer see them.

Spencer felt a burden had been lifted from him. Overjoyed, he shouted, "I did it, Yes! I did it!" He shook his fist in the air. "I brought them back together, yes…yes!"

"Mr. Aubreys, are you okay?"

Spencer turned quickly to find Allen standing under an umbrella about twenty feet from him, a flashlight in hand.

Taking a deep breath and shaking his head, he replied, "Yes, Allen, I couldn't be better."

"Are you sure you're okay?" Allen asked again, appearing confused. "You dropped your coat on the ground behind you."

Spencer looked back and saw his coat lying on the ground at the exact spot where Katherine and Sam had stood together a mere second ago. He walked over and picked it up, realizing that it was now soaking wet. Beginning to tremble and hurting even more from the cold air and rain, he walked back to Allen.

"How did you know that I was out here?"

"I didn't. One of our guests said he heard someone calling for someone down here and thought they needed help. So, here I am. You are shaking, Mr. Aubreys. We need to get you inside."

"Yes, Allen, I agree." Gazing back into the darkness, but seeing nothing, he followed Allen into the Inn.

CHAPTER 19
The Final Chapter

After taking a hot shower, Spencer sat in front of the fire in his room, wrapped in his house robe and blanket, trying to warm his chilled, exhausted body. Thinking about Sam and their journey out of the mountain, he now knew what happened almost a century and a half ago on a night just like this. With the final chapter of their story in mind, he couldn't wait to write it. Fatigued, his body yearned for rest, but he knew the final chapter had to be written first.

There was a knock at the door. Opening it, he found Allen standing with a tray.

"Mr. Aubreys, I brought you some hot tea. I thought it would warm your insides."

"Please come in. I'm sure it'll help."

Allen carried the tea to the bar and poured it. "You looked pretty bad out there. Are you sure you're okay?" He handed Spencer a cup of tea.

"I'm fine now, Allen." Spencer knew that standing in the cold rain with no coat and shouting to himself looked strange, so he decided to question him.

"Do you believe in ghosts, or do you think there could be spirits here that may be wandering around, searching for someone in their past?"

Allen stared at Spencer for a few seconds and then smiled. "It's hard for me not to imagine these hallways and rooms weren't once filled with romance, laughter, and even tragedy. You only have to walk these hallways late at night by yourself to get the feeling that you're in another time and place. Sometimes one gets the feeling that we're the ones intruding on someone else's space."

Relieved, Spencer sighed. *Maybe there's someone here who doesn't think I'm crazy after all.* "Thank you, Allen."

"Is there more I can do?" Allen asked, standing at the fireplace.

"No, I'm good now. I need to outline a chapter for a book. Please know that I appreciate the tea. Just add it to my room tab."

"No, it's our treat. Just wanted to make sure your stay with us is pleasant. Call me if you need more." He let himself out the door.

Spencer declined dinner with Elaine and Bernice so he could outline his final chapter. He scheduled to meet them later to give Elaine his first draft for her to review. Sitting at his table and listening to the pouring rain outside, he began to write.

The words took on a life of their own. Page after page, words flowed and fell in place. Words telling the story about the love between a young girl and boy who knew each other for only two weeks, yet loved each other enough to last a lifetime and beyond. Just as fast as the War Between the States had brought them together, it had torn them apart. Her love, will and passion had kept the love of her life alive until they could once again be together eternally, if only in another realm.

Spencer finished writing the chapter and felt emotionally drained, knowing that he'd probably never again be able to write with the same intensity and emotion. He yearned to understand why he was chosen to tell the story of Katherine and Samuel. Leaning back in his chair, he sighed and thought of his own situation.

Maybe it was the loneliness that I live with every day, feeling that something is missing in my life while longing for Miriam, unsure how to get back to her. Did Katherine, sensing the pain and disappointment in my life, see a way to connect with me? Somehow, we shared mutual emotions, and I was in the right place at the right time and she was able to connect with me. One thing for sure, I now have a different outlook and respect for the love two people can share.

Spencer got up and paced the floor feeling antsy and thinking. *There's something else I need to take care of.* The squeeze ball he had thrown across the room caught his attention. It still lay on the floor. He reached for it, but then decided to let it lie. Instead, he reached for his cell phone and dialed.

"Hello," Miriam paused. "Spencer, is that you?"

"Yes, it is." He kept his voice low. "What're you up to tonight?"

"I just made myself a cup of hot chocolate, curled up on the sofa listening to the rain, trying to read myself to sleep." She paused and asked, "What about you? What're you doing?"

Spencer smiled, imagining her curled up on the couch reading, with the fireplace lit, exactly as he had often seen her do. "I've just finished writing the outline for my book. And I'm also listening to the rain while sitting in front of the fireplace in my room."

"No one can ever accuse us of running off with the social crowd, can they?" Miriam laughed.

Spencer was glad the tension during their last phone call had disappeared. He sat down on the sofa and ran his fingers through his hair, trying to find the words he wanted to say. "No, they can't. In fact, you and I never did well in crowds. We never demanded a lot of entertainment; usually just being together was enough."

"Why did you call?"

"I want to apologize for shouting at you last night when we spoke. Also, I have something on my mind I need to talk to you about." Spencer waited for her response, unsure if he should speak openly.

She answered with a different and softer tone in her voice, "I'm listening."

He took a deep breath. "Since being here in Abingdon this week and getting my mind off day-to-day distractions, my job loss and our separation, things have happened to make me think about you and me. I know that I haven't been the easiest person to live with over the last twenty-seven years. When I think about how you've put up with me, I admire you even more for it. Miriam, do you remember the times we used to take long weekend getaways and travel all over the country; weekend picnics with the kids on the Parkway; or the times we had to juggle schedules to get two kids off in different directions every day? Our life was full of challenges, but we never let it come between us."

Spencer paused in case Miriam wanted to say something. When she didn't respond, he continued. "Do you remember the first time we met at the Chamber meeting and how you made me laugh all evening? For years you have brought laughter and so much joy to my life that it's hard for me to imagine my life without you."

"What are you trying to say, Spencer?" she asked.

"You know me, I am better at writing words than speaking them." He took a deep breath. "Miriam, ever since I left you, I've been trying to find a way to get back to you. I don't want to give up on us. I want to see you smile again. I want you to make me laugh. And I want another dance with you."

He waited through silence, and then continued. "Can we give us another chance? Not to go back to what it was but to make it better? Maybe it won't be easy, but I want to try." He eased further back into the sofa, relieved that the words he longed to say were said. Spencer waited for Miriam's reply, hoping that her response would be what he wanted to hear, but willing to concede for her sake, if she chose differently. There was none.

Finally, he said, "Are you still there?"

When she replied, he realized she was crying.

"I've wanted to get back to you, too, but I didn't know how. I went along with the separation, hoping we'd both realize that what we had was important. I know things haven't been good between us and that I've also been part of the blame." She sobbed,

"Yes, Spencer, I want to try to make it better, too. And I love you even more for not giving up on us."

He felt relieved. "You do realize I am unemployed, and the job market doesn't look good right now, don't you?"

"Well, let's see," she said, sniffing a couple of times. "If you are going to be the homemaker, then for me there's no more housework or laundry and a full course dinner every evening would be okay"

They both laughed.

"I'll start looking for work again on Monday." He stood and started walking around the room.

"I wish I could be there with you right now," Miriam added.

"I wish you could be here with me, too. You would love this place. I'll bring you back here soon."

"Well, what do we need to do?"

"First, let's call the lawyers and fire them. And how about dinner out with me tomorrow night? Your choice, and maybe with a little urging I might be persuaded to spend the night with you."

"Hmm, I look forward to our first date back together."

Spencer could already see her smiling. "Then I'll leave as soon as possible in the morning. I'll call you when I get back to Charlottesville."

"I'm looking forward to it."

"Miriam, I don't want to end our conversation. But I need to run downstairs and give Elaine the outline of my story. I promised to meet her in the lobby at nine."

"Did you get the ending to your story?"

"I'll share it with you over dinner tomorrow. In the meantime, enjoy your book and read yourself to sleep."

"I will…love you. Be careful driving home."

"Can't wait to see you, Miriam. Love you, too."

Feeling a burden was lifted from him, Spencer gathered his outline. Still exhausted, but excited, he went downstairs and found Elaine and Bernice sitting in the lobby.

When he walked in, Elaine said, "You missed a good dinner with us tonight."

"I bet I did. But I wanted to get the draft finished on the story I wrote this week. Can't wait to see what you think about it." He handed it to her.

Holding it with both hands, she looked at it. "I'll start reading it tonight."

"You said you needed to talk to me about something?" he asked, anticipating her questions about his telling Bernice that he had encountered a ghost.

"You look exhausted. Why don't you go up and rest? I'll come by around ten in the morning, if that works for you. Maybe we can do brunch before you leave."

"Sure, that would be good. By the way, the trip down to the Inn has been good for me. I appreciate your recommending it." He turned to Bernice, who sat staring and not saying a word. "And thank you for your help. I couldn't have written this story without it."

"Glad to have helped," she nodded with a frown on her face.

"Good night, I'll see you in the morning."

"Get some rest," Elaine reminded him.

Spencer stepped over to the front desk to speak to a night-shift clerk. "Is your gift shop still open? I need to pick up a razor."

"No, Mr. Aubreys, it's not." She reached under the counter. "But I have razors here at the desk."

"Thanks." He walked away.

He could imagine Elaine and Bernice talking about him. *I'm surprised Elaine didn't say something to me tonight. I'm sure she wanted to know where this ghost talk was coming from. I have no way to prove that Katherine does exist, but I'll just have to deal with it in the morning.*

With the gas logs casting a glow over the bedroom again, Spencer sat on the sofa listening to the rain fall. His mind relaxed and he realized how much better he felt since the burden of his separation from Miriam had been lifted. He thought of Katherine and Sam and the love they had for each other. *Did their time of longing for each other actually go on for a century and a half? Or was it more like the blink of an eye to them? How could two people who knew each other for only two weeks find themselves so much in love?* Then he remembered the first time he had seen Miriam at the Chamber reception. *I knew when I first met her that I wanted her. I wanted to hold her, dance with her and love her. I guess real love is often tested by disappointments and time.*

Sleep began to beckon him, so he turned off the gas logs and practically fell into bed. Remembering the room door was not locked, he decided that it didn't matter. *I'm too tired to go down the hall and lock it. Nobody will bother me here anyway.* He drifted into sleep.

CHAPTER 20
The Flower

Slowly opening his eyes, Spencer surveyed his surroundings. Sunlight shined through the window of the open curtains. Remembering nothing since he had gone to bed, he turned over to look at the clock and saw that it was already nine o'clock.

Suddenly, he heard a voice calling from the sitting room entrance. "Hello, I'm the room maid. Is anybody in here?"

"Yes, I am! What do you need?" he shouted back.

"Nothing, Mr. Aubreys, your door was open. I thought you might have already checked out and left. Sorry to bother you."

"No, that's fine. I didn't lock the door last night. But I'm sure I closed it."

"I'll shut it for you, Mr. Aubreys. Take your time getting up and leaving."

"Thank you. I'll be out within the hour," he replied before he heard the door close.

He strolled into the sitting room and locked the door. Turning to go take a shower, he noticed a flower on the table, the same kind of flower that Katherine picked during two of their visits together. It lay on his laptop. He picked it up and brushed the pink petals and yellow center with his fingertips, thinking of how Katherine brushed one when she held it. *Perhaps the maid that was in earlier laid it on the laptop*, he thought.

After a quick shower, he observed himself in the mirror. Focusing on his five day-old-beard and knowing it was going to be a challenge, he began to shave.

Glancing at his watch, he realized he had to meet Elaine downstairs in fifteen minutes. Hurriedly packing his clothes, he crammed his laptop into his satchel and reached for the flower lying on the table. He couldn't help but feel bittersweet about leaving. He had arrived stressed out and feeling hopeless, wondering where his life was going. Now, leaving, he felt refreshed, energized and ready for whatever challenges may lie ahead. He closed the door softly behind him, reminded that his life had been changed.

At the front desk he saw two woman busy shuffling and filing papers. He approached them. "Good morning, ladies."

"Good morning, Mr. Aubreys. What can I do for you?" Julia asked, resting her arms on the counter.

Setting his bags down, he said, "I'm checking out. What do I need to do?"

"Nothing, Mr. Aubreys. Elaine came by and covered your bill. She and Bernice just went down the hallway."

"Thanks, I'll go find her. She's a great lady, isn't she?"

"Yes, I have to agree. I met her through her sister here in Abingdon. I always look forward to her visits. The Inn is one of her favorite places."

"I can understand why," he responded.

"Mr. Aubreys, I hope your visit with us has been a memorable experience."

Spencer smiled. "Yes, Julia; it has been quite memorable." He thought about all that had happened to him, knowing no one would ever believe him if he told them.

"Would you like Allen to drive your car around to the front?"

Elaine walked up. "Good morning, Spencer. You look well rested and refreshed this morning. And you've shaved your beard!"

"I thought it was about time I cleaned up," he chuckled. "By the way, what do you need to talk to me about?"

"Why don't you leave your bags here? We can walk down the hallway and talk."

"Sure." Spencer handed his car keys to Julia. "If Allen comes by, ask him to bring my car around. I'll be back in a few minutes."

He knew Elaine was going to bring up the ghost encounter he had shared with Bernice.

Walking down the hallway, Elaine spoke, "Spencer, I read your outline last night. It is one of the most interesting stories I have read in years. I think you have a great chance of getting someone's attention with it."

"Thank you, Elaine. You always had confidence in me. I appreciate you for that."

"The history during the Civil War era, a young girl and boy's romance, and how you portrayed their love for each other—what inspired you to write that? The story seemed so real. I couldn't put the manuscript down once I started it."

Walking past the Garden View hallway, they saw Bernice staring through the window. Seeing them, she beckoned to them in an excited whisper. "Elaine, come quick and watch this!"

With whetted curiosity, Spencer led the way toward her.

"Look!" Bernice exclaimed, pointing out the window. "I just saw a young girl with auburn hair wearing a long, pale-blue dress and dancing with a young boy dressed in a Confederate uniform. They were dancing on the walkway bridge over the water."

Elaine and Spencer looked out, but neither saw anyone. Elaine asked, "Where did they go?"

"I don't know. I only turned my head for a second. They couldn't have walked away that fast."

Elaine glanced at Spencer, and then with a quick, sly wink, she asked, "Did you see anyone?"

Trying to hide a grin, he shrugged his shoulders and spread his empty hands. "I didn't see anyone."

Bernice spoke in her own defense. "I'm telling you, a young girl and boy were dancing on the bridge. I stood watching them for several minutes before you walked up."

Spencer loved every minute of it as he watched Elaine's veiled attempt to reassure Bernice that she believed her.

Back into the lobby, Bernice went to the front desk and began to tell Julia about her experience.

Spencer turned to Elaine and asked, "What did you need to talk to me about?"

She smiled, with somewhat of a twinkle in her eyes, and said, "Nothing. Not anymore."

Spencer picked up his bags. "Then I'm out of here. I need to get back to Charlottesville. I have a date with a beautiful woman this evening."

"Anybody I know?" Elaine asked.

"Maybe." He winked at her.

With that mystery hanging in the air, he left.

A few minutes later, Spencer drove to the exit to turn into the street. He paused to pick up the flower lying on his dash and whirled it between a finger and thumb, still wondering how it came to be in his room. Glancing in his rearview mirror for one last look at the Inn, his heart skipped a beat as his gaze lifted to the third floor balcony where Sam had been a patient. There were Katherine and Sam, arms around each other and waving to him. He turned his head quickly to look back, but they were gone. There was no one there. He smiled, laid the flower back on the dash and drove onto the street.

Shaking his head but happy in his knowledge they were together, he looked both ways before pressing on the accelerator and heading on to his renewed life.

CHAPTER 21

Eight Months Later

Spencer reached for his stress-relief squeeze ball and tossed it into the air a couple of times, then laid it down and picked up his suitcase. He went from the bedroom to the kitchen, stopped and pressed the telephone button to leave a message.

"Hello, this is Spencer. I am leaving for a few days with a beautiful woman whom I intend to spoil and have fun with. If you need me, leave a message, and I may or may not return the call. Thank you."

He turned to find Miriam, who was grinning at him. "What do you think people who call here and listen to that message will think?"

He placed a finger on his chin, rolled his eyes up and grinned back. "They might say that old married, middle-aged couple actually knows how to have fun."

"You know, I think you're probably right," Miriam said as she stepped closer, clasping her hands around his neck. "I am so glad we're back together. I can't imagine what my life would be like if we hadn't worked things out. I love you more than ever."

Putting his finger under her chin, he tilted her face up. "I have to agree with you. It gets better every day. Come on. Let's get going or the kids will beat us to Abingdon."

"Do you think they'll be surprised to learn we're renewing our vows in the gazebo at the Inn?"

"It's the least we can do after what we've put them through during our separation. Besides, we're doing it for us. Hopefully, it will have a lasting impression on their marriages, too." He pulled her close and kissed her.

A few minutes later on US 29 South, Spencer's cell phone rang. "Hello, Spencer here."

"Hi, Spencer. This is Elaine. Got your message off your phone, and I like it. Where're you two off to?"

"I am taking Miriam to the Inn in Abingdon for a long weekend."

"I'm sure she'll enjoy it. You two are special people and deserve each other. Have lots of fun. The reason I called is that I wanted to give you an update on your book. It has been sent to the printer and should be ready for release shortly. Your publisher wanted to know when your next book will be available."

"I won't start another one until this fall. Miriam is not working at school this summer. So I'm going to try to spoil her as much as I can." He winked at Miriam; she returned a smile.

"I am so proud of both of you. You two have fun. We'll talk once you get back home. Also, I want you to know that I think you were very generous sending part of your book advance to Christine Hudson."

"The story I wrote was about her great-grandmother. Without her help and Katherine's diary, I wouldn't have been able to finish the book."

"From what you told me, I'm sure they could use the money. She'll be pleasantly surprised at what you've done. Enjoy your trip."

"Thank you, Elaine, for believing in me and being a great friend. Bye."

Spencer turned his attention to Miriam, "I know you'll enjoy the Inn."

"I'm sure I will. Do you think we may meet up with Katherine Broadwater again?"

"No, I think she's where she wants to be now."

"And where would that be?"

"Spending her time with the love of her life somewhere in eternity. Wherever that is."

Spencer moved his hand from the steering wheel and reached for Miriam's hand. "Samuel and Katherine waited practically forever to get back to each other. I think I understand why." He held Miriam's hand as they headed toward Abingdon.

In Lebanon, Kathy answered the doorbell and signed for a package from the FedEx driver. Taking it to her grandmother, she said, "Grandma, I bet it's Spencer's book."

Excitedly tearing the package open, Christine could hardly wait to see the story of her own great-grandmother. "That's it. Look at the beautiful cover!"

As she showed it to Kathy, something fluttered to the floor. Kathy stooped to pick up the piece of paper and exclaimed, "Grandma, it's a check!"

"Why would he send a check? Let me see."

Kathy screamed, "Grandma, you'll never believe this. Look! Does it say ten thousand dollars?"

Christine gasped as her granddaughter handed her the check with a note paper clipped to it. Her hands were shaking as she read it out loud.

"Dear Mrs. Christine Katherine Hudson,

It was a pleasure meeting you and your granddaughter Kathy in November. Enclosed is a part of the advance royalties I am receiving from the book I wrote about your great-grandmother, Katherine Broadwater. I hope this money will help you, and maybe help Kathy and David keep their home. I will send more as I receive it. Never have I enjoyed writing or learning about someone as I have your great-grandmother. Her life, her beauty and her passion for Sam was a story that had to be told.

The note in her diary from her mother was so appropriate: 'Someday, someone will look back and read what you have written and will know what a beautiful and wonderful young lady you are.'

Best of luck to you and thank you for your help.

Spencer Aubreys"

Julia was busy at the front desk at the Inn when a young couple stepped up to check out.

"Hi, Todd and Judi. How are our new bride and groom doing today?" She put down her paperwork and stepped up to the counter to help them. "I hear your wedding in the gazebo was absolutely beautiful."

"It was wonderful," the new bride beamed, holding onto her husband's arm. "The weather was great, the reception went well, and everyone at the Inn made sure everything went off without a hitch."

"We know how to do weddings around here," Julia said proudly.

"And sending the young girl to our room to play her violin for us last night was a perfect touch," Judi said.

"We didn't send her," Julia said, worry creeping into her voice. "Maybe your parents did."

"No, we asked," Judi said.

"Hmmm, what did she look like?" Julia asked.

"Tall, slim with long, black hair," Todd said.

"She was dressed in a long, old-fashioned black-and-white lace dress," Judi added. "She played beautifully—she even cried, it was so beautiful."

"I don't know who she was," Julia said. "Did she say her name?"

"No," Judi answered, and then paused thoughtfully. "But she reminded me of that girl we met here last fall when we checked out the gazebo. She was with that writer, yes, Spencer Aubreys, I think." She turned to Todd. "You know, honey, the young girl with long, auburn hair and wore that blue dress that I liked. She spoke with that really southern accent. I can't remember her name. Stillwater, Broadwater, something to do with water."

"Katherine Broadwater?" Julia asked, the hairs on her arms standing up.

"That was it," Todd said. "That violin player reminded us of her." He signed the receipt and folded his copy and stuffed it in his pocket.

"But anyway, the music was beautiful, and we plan on spending every anniversary here," Judi said, looking lovingly up at her husband.

"Well sure," Julia said, fumbling with a reply. "Thank you all for coming to the Inn. We will look forward to seeing you when you return."

The couple left and Julia stood staring at the door, thinking of Spencer and how hard he tried to convince everyone that Katherine did exist. Now Todd and Judi just confirmed that she did.

Just then Allen walked up from the side and said, "Hi, Julia."

She jumped at the sound, scattering papers everywhere.

"Sorry, Julia," Allen said, bending down to pick up the papers. "I thought you saw me." He looked at her just standing there, looking a little pale. "Are you okay, Julia? You look like you've seen a ghost."

9380058R0

Made in the USA
Charleston, SC
07 September 2011